A. D. Emery left secondary school without any academic qualifications. However, whilst playing in a band for some years, he attended evening classes, eventually achieving a BSc in Physics. He started working in engineering, then moving into electromagnetic research, which led him into computer programming. He now lives with his wife in South Lincolnshire. His children have left home and now live in various parts of the country. Although, the three youngest grandchildren live close, and he enjoys their visits. A passion for writing, despite dyslexia, developed in later years.

To my grandchildren and great grandchildren.

A.D. Emery

HIDDEN AGENDA

AUSTIN MACAULEY PUBLISHERS®

LONDON • CAMBRIDGE • NEW YORK • SHARJAH

A CIP catalogue record for this title is available from the British Library.

ISBN 9781035874903 (Paperback)
ISBN 9781035874910 (ePub e-book)

www.austinmacauley.com

First Published 2024
Austin Macauley Publishers Ltd®
1 Canada Square
Canary Wharf
London
E14 5AA

Chapter 1

Slowly, I became aware that my name was being called. I wasn't startled; it was more of a slow realisation I was no longer dreaming. Although thinking about it, I don't remember whether or not I had actually been dreaming. A voice faintly impinged itself on my subconscious. I was standing at, or rather, leaning on the starboard side of 'Destiny's' bridge, having wedged myself into a corner for support.

During the outward journey, the rocking motion of the tug and pitching of the horizon had had a very soporific effect on me. This, combined with the fact that, as the trip had progressed, the periods of light sporadic conversation had slowly decreased in frequency, until their incidence had reached zero.

Altogether, the combined movement and the total lack of conversation had caused me to become lost within my own thoughts; eventually, I had drifted into a state of being half asleep, neither awake nor fully asleep—just resting my eyes.

Once again, the voice imposed itself over my thoughts, "Paul, will you take this wheel?"

In response to this intrusion, I moved and stretched.

"Come on, Paul. Wake up and get your backside over here and take this wheel!" This time, Dave was shouting at me.

As my brain started to refocus on reality, I became aware that the usual penetrating vibration and heavy pounding of the massive marine diesel engine that powered Destiny had moderated to almost silence. Rousing myself to try and establish what all the shouting was about, I realised that Jim, the captain, had left the bridge and Dave was the only person left on the bridge, apart from myself, that is.

Seeing that I was at last responding. Dave shouted again, "Will you get yourself into gear and come over here and take this wheel?" This time, I noticed that his voice had developed a slight edge of irritation in it, which in hindsight was probably a bit of an understatement.

"Sorry. Don't get wound up," I mumbled, rubbing my eyes to bring them back into focus. At the same time, I moved across to the centre of the bridge, where Dave was standing in front of the wheel.

"Are you awake now?" He asked, more out of sarcasm than genuine interest.

"Yes, of course, I was only daydreaming." I replied, still rubbing my eyes.

I stretched again and smiled at Dave, "There, I'm wide awake now." Dave looked at me with a disbelieving expression on his face and didn't return my smile.

"Okay, if you say so. Get hold of this wheel. I'm going to give you an instantaneous lesson in steering. Try turning her to starboard," Dave instructed, after I had taken my stance in front of the wheel.

"Which side is starboard?"

"Right!" Snapped Dave harshly.

Judging it would probably be best if I refrained from commenting on his disgruntled manner, I obediently turned the wheel half a turn to starboard. Nothing happened.

"Give it another half a turn," encouraged Dave.

I gave it another half a turn this time. 'Destiny' started to turn.

"Now turn her back."

This time, I turned the wheel half a turn to port; again, nothing happened. Anticipating Dave, I gave it another half-turn, and Destiny's bow stopped turning.

"She's still pointing in the wrong direction," I observed.

"I suppose I should be pleased you're awake enough to notice it. Now reverse what you just did." Dave instructed, although there was still a sarcastic tone in his voice.

Again, I turned the wheel a turn to port, and then back again, this time 'Destiny' came round onto her original heading.

"Got the feel of it?" Dave asked.

"I think so," I replied hesitantly, trying to sound confident.

"The wheel's got about half a turn of play in it," Dave emphasised, "which means the rudder has the equivalent amount of side-to-side slack. You'll probably be able to feel it as a sort of wagging in this weather. You'll soon get used to it, though."

"Thanks. Is that all there is to it?"

"No, but it's all I've got time to show you for now. Keep her on that heading," Dave added, pointing at the compass. "So, she's pointing into the waves whilst I go down and check the engine. Its temperature doesn't look right, and without John down there, I can't take any chances. I've reduced her speed, so the steering has become a bit sluggish, and she'll tend to try and do her own thing."

"Right. I'm sure I can handle it." The words were designed to give me confidence rather than Dave.

Outside, the low, dark grey clouds streaked across the sky ahead of the driving wind. Although I had been absentmindedly watching the waves for some time, I hadn't realised how much the weather had deteriorated. Earlier, 'Destiny' had been sedately riding the waves, but now, each time she crested a wave, she jarred as the bow plunged into the wave's trough. This resulted in me feeling the rudder being buffeted from side to side through my hands on the wheel. Each time the rudder took up the slack in the steering mechanism. The wheel jerked, and I tried to rip the spokes of the wheel out of my hand.

I remembered thinking, "That this must be what Dave called wagging."

Determined not to make a complete hash of this apparently simple task, I tightened my grip on the wheel and looked down at the compass to check the heading. Suddenly, whilst I was distracted by this split-second task, Destiny's bow pitched over another wave crest and crashed into the wave's trough on the other side. Instinctively, I ducked as the Southern Atlantic Ocean smashed against the glass of the bridge. Unfortunately, this momentary distraction caused my grip on the wheel to relax, and the wheel suddenly kicked out of my hands and spun round. Instantly, 'Destiny' lurched sideways and started to yaw off her heading.

"Hold that wheel steady!" Dave shouted as he reached the top of the companionway, down to the engine room. As 'Destiny' rolled, Dave staggered sideways and banged his shoulder against the side of the companionway; this caused him to swear as he disappeared down the stairs towards the engine room below.

"I'm trying to!" I shouted back, "But I wasn't expecting that."

As I tried to grab the spinning spokes of the wheel, they striped the skin off my knuckles. It seemed like a lifetime before I got hold of the wheel again, but I suspect it was only a matter of a few seconds. Having gotten hold of it, I spun it around in the opposite direction to try and bring 'Destiny' back on the original heading.

"This is more difficult than I expected." I gasped. The lack of a reply told me I was speaking to myself as Dave was now out of earshot in the engine room.

Watching the compass needle swing back past the required heading, I realised I had overreacted. Immediately I spun the wheel back the other way. You can probably guess what happened for the next two or three minutes. 'Destiny' yawed from side to side until I worked out how much to anticipate each swing and compensate with the opposite rudder. Eventually the compass needle came to rest, pointing approximately in the right direction again.

Ten minutes or so later, Dave reappeared, wiping his hands on some cotton waste.

"You had a bit of fun whilst I was below," Dave observed. "This weather's deteriorated quite a lot since we left the island."

"That must be the understatement of the day," I remarked, returning his earlier sarcasm.

As if on cue, another wave leapt over the bow and smashed into the bridge. Again, my self-preservation reflex action cut in. However, this time Dave was close enough to grab the wheel from me before it had time to kick round.

"You'll soon get used to that!" He grinned at me, "Here, wipe that blood of the deck before Jim comes back, and also your knuckles." He added as he handed me the bundle of cotton waste. I was quite surprised to see how much blood had dripped on to the deck, as I didn't think I had damaged myself that much.

"I'm not sure I want to get used to it, though. How much longer do we have to keep this up?" I asked.

"Take the wheel for a second and I'll check."

I grabbed the wheel again and changed the subject away from my instinctive response for self-preservation.

Dave went to the back of the bridge and looked out at the activity on 'Destiny's' rear deck.

"Another five or ten minutes should do it," he replied, as he returned and relieved me of the wheel.

'Destiny', an old ocean-going tug, had been brought round into the wind by Dave just before handing the wheel over to me earlier. Subsequently, Dave and I were struggling, so it seemed to me, to maintain its almost stationary position and heading over the roller-coasting waves. Trying to protect the rear deck from as much of the bad weather as possible for the necessary few minutes. In addition, the water was also streaming over the side from an increasing number of engulfing waves, plus the spray being whipped off the wave tops by the driving wind, all of which combined into a streaming torrent across the heaving and pitching rear deck, contributing to the general discomfort of all those outside.

Chapter 2

Attached to a safety line and standing in the lee of 'Destiny's' rust-streaked bridge, Captain Jim McNally clutched the handrail of the bulkhead ladder with one hand and held a small prayer book, wrapped in a plastic bag, in the other. The continuously heaving deck made it impossible for Jim to read the prayer book, which didn't really make any difference, as he knew the words off by heart. However, the prayer book itself was extremely necessary, it was Jim's prop. Just as an actor needs a costume to help him get the full essence of the character, he's playing; Jim needed the support that the pray book provided to get him through the committal proceedings. It took about ten minutes for Jim to conclude the brief service, but for Jim, it always seemed like a lifetime. Jim always felt the committal service was a necessary full stop to life. Even if the screaming wind precluded the rest of the crew from hearing a single word.

Also attached to the tug by safety lines were Josh and Phil; these were the other two members of the tug's crew. They huddled in their waterproofs at the stern of the tug, waiting for Jim to finish. When they saw, rather than heard, Jim utters the last amen, they lifted the first of two plain bright yellow coffins and pushed it over the side, quickly following it with the second coffin. Immediately, both coffins hesitantly floated on the surface of the water for a few seconds, then they were gone, swallowed by the tug's wake. All traces are instantly erased by the driving wind and raging waves. All three of them watched for a few seconds as the coffins disappeared below the surging water.

"Let's get back to the island; there's no point in staying out in this any longer than necessary," Jim shouted at the other crew members. Again, Jim's words couldn't be heard, but the crew on deck knew what to do from experience and scrambled up the pitching deck and tumbled through the bulkhead door to get undercover. Josh and Phil made their way through to the crew's mess, whilst Jim climbed up to the bridge.

On reaching the bridge, he removed his sodden oilskins and quietly took stock of the situation.

"You can go down below and join the others in the mess if you want to, Paul," Jim said quietly as he took the wheel from me.

"No. I think I'd like to stay up here, provided it's alright with you."

Jim nodded his agreement.

Dave opened the engine's throttles up, and the penetrating vibration and heavy pounding of the massive V12 diesel returned. 'Destiny' started to gain speed, and as soon as the steering became responsive again, Jim checked the compass and turned Destiny onto the required heading, to take them back to the island. A sombre silence engulfed the bridge as the three of us stared out at the bleak wind-torn ocean.

'Destiny' ploughed on, shrouded in silence it was as if the tug was manned by zombies. Time drifted slowly past. After a while, I seem to remember wondering if I was getting used to the waves crashing against the bridge, or if they were slowly subsiding.

Abruptly, well, at least it made me jump. As if a radio had been switched on, Jim's voice cut through the silence, which had pervaded throughout 'Destiny' for some half an hour or so.

"I think the weather seems to be abating," Jim remarked.

At least, it confirmed my thoughts that I wasn't getting used to the buffeting or becoming desensitised, and in fact the waves were subsiding.

Verbal silence returned for a few more moments before Jim spoke again, "Thanks for helping out, Paul. Sorry, your first trip has turned out to be such a rough one."

Picking up on the revival of conversation, Dave commented, "Sorry, I shouted at you, Paul. I think you handled it reasonably well back there, considering it's the first time you've been on a ship's bridge at sea—and a rough sea at that."

"Glad I was able to help. However, I don't think I'd like to do it on a regular basis, in this kind of weather anyway."

"It's usually a bit more dignified than just tossing coffins over the stern," Jim continued. "Generally, we set a couple planks up and slide them in gently with at least some sense of dignity."

"Which is a lot more than they got towards the end of their life," I added.

"That's true," the other two concurred in unison.

Again, silence descended over the bridge. The circumstances of the voyage seemed to make light conversation difficult and inappropriate, leaving silence as the best compromise.

Eventually the outline of the island's coast showed on the radar. The dark clouds and failing light caused the green glow from the radar's CRT screen to flicker eerily on the three faces as they stared out into the growing gloom. Jim's weather-beaten face looked tense, weary, and tired. Only the slight relaxation of his features revealed his relief at sighting the two buoys acting as sentinels for the harbour entrance.

Half an hour later, the crew had anchored 'Destiny' in the centre of the bay, which formed the island's natural harbour. It was now evening. During the three hours, or so, of the return journey, the storm had blown itself out, and the odd star could be seen through the rifts in the racing clouds. A stiff breeze, which passed for normal calm weather on the island, now blew steadily from the Southwest.

"I'm glad that's over." Jim voiced the thoughts of all of them on the bridge, "It's funny how none of the crew like making these trips, least of all me, but it's the reason why we're here, and I suppose we'll just have to put up with it. Although knowing you've got to do, it doesn't make it any easier."

The homecoming—if you can call it home, living on 'Destiny' in the middle of a bay—was always a relief. All the members of the crew had originally been given the option of living in relatively comfortable accommodation on the island, but their imagination and fear had hyped that prospect into something to be avoided at all costs. Consequently, they never left the tug unless absolutely necessary—hoping the moat provided by the bay's water would provide them protection from the horrors of their imagination. Jim was usually the only one who ever ventured further than the island's jetty.

"I hope John's sprained ankle will soon be improved," I remarked. "Although he seems to be hopping around the mess sprightly enough now. Are you certain you really did need me on this trip?"

"Of course we did." Dave replied. "Come on, how would John have managed in that weather? He wouldn't have been able to stand in the engine room all that time, even if it had been calm weather. Let alone looking after the engine during the stuff we had out there this afternoon. He'd have been a danger to himself."

"It's just that I had a sudden slight feeling that I was set up."

"I can assure you; we didn't know the weather was going to be as bad as that when we left," Jim asserted. Then I quickly changed the subject before someone asked about weather forecasts.

Jim then added, "Paul, why don't you stay on board the tug tonight? It'll help disperse the gloom that seems to be a characteristic of the evenings after one of these trips. You know—someone different to talk to and take their minds of the day's events. I'm sure Josh will have cooked enough dinner to give you some."

"You can use the spare bunk, and it'll also save someone having to get the dinghy out tonight," encouraged Dave. "And as another incentive, Jim's got an unopened bottle of Johnny Walker whisky, which I'm sure needs some attention."

"With that kind of bribery, how can I refuse? Thanks. Come on then, let's have a party and get that bottle open before I change my mind."

The three of them left the bridge and joined John, Josh, and Phil in the mess room. Silence descended again.

However, this time it wasn't the depressing sombre silence of earlier, but a joyful few moments as they scoffed the steak pie and chips that Josh had cooked during their return.

The mess room wasn't a separate dining room; it was just one end of the biggest cabin on the tug; it stretched from under the bridge to about halfway between the bridge and the bow. The table, with its raised edge to prevent things sliding off when the sea was rough, was a bit tight for six to sit round but comfortable for the normal complement of five. Its ceiling, the underside of the forward deck and bridge floor, was six feet six inches from the floor at its highest point. However, the deck supporting beams that traversed the room every two feet or so made it necessary for me, at six foot two inches, to walk with a stoop. If I forgot to stoop when moving around, the beams soon reminded me. Each member of the crew had found his own niche within the cabin, which all the others recognised as his and respected whatever small personalisation had been made.

After the pie and chips had been devoured, Josh brought pudding in from the galley—baked jam roly-poly.

"All home made," announced Josh, grinning at me.

"He may have made the roly-poly, but the custard comes ready made out of a five-gallon drum," Jim whispered in my ear.

Silence descended again until the plates were empty. Then, as if by magic, bottles of assorted alcoholic beverages instantly appeared from various cubbyholes and stowage lockers and the glasses were filled. Jim brought out two glasses.

"One for you and one for me," he mumbled at me as he placed them on table, and shot a generous slug of Johnny Walker whisky into both of them.

Jim stood up and raised his glass. "Here's to Paul—for whatever he did to help us," he announced.

"Cheers," came the response.

"Thanks," I replied. "It was nothing."

"We know that," they all replied in chorus and then laughed.

"I should have expected a comment like that, or at least seen it coming."

The murmur of conversation filled the cabin. As I remember it, the talk drifted from football to rugby, through a hundred and one other things, as the alcohol relaxed our minds. Suddenly the conversation landed on the subject of murders.

"You know, this AIDS thing makes the perfect murder almost easy," announced John.

"How's that?" Jim asked.

"You know, you're right," I replied. "It's simple. Bash them on the head from behind, so they're out cold. Give them a quick injection with contaminated blood. Pinch their wallet to make it look like a robbery, and no one would know."

"Hang on, where's this contaminated blood going to come from without someone knowing?" Dave cut in.

"Find someone with AIDS and take some," Phil stated.

"Or what about breaking into a lab or hospital." added Josh.

"But that's the point," Jim argued. "If you involve a third person or break in somewhere, you don't have the perfect murder anymore. If more than one person is involved, you can bet yourself that someone will open their mouth, or you'll be overheard discussing it."

"That's true," I added. "They may be slow and appear dim, but if there's any sort of connection, the police usually manage to eventually find it some way or another. No, I think I'll agree with Jim. The more complicated the method, the less perfect the murder."

"Anyway, John, who do you want to bump off?" asked Jim.

"You, of course, I want to be captain of this magnificent vessel."

They all turned and looked at John. His face held a serious look for about ten seconds; it then broke into a grin and ended in a convulsed guffaw.

"People have been killed for a lot less," he added after he had stopped laughing.

"I'd only have to kick your bad leg, and that would soon sort you out," Jim replied with a funny sort of smirk, which was the result of trying to keep a straight face and trying not to laugh.

"You wouldn't be that cruel to John, would you, Jim?" I sniggered.

"You just wait until he tries to murder me. However, if he does succeed, I'll make sure my ghost kicks his leg every hour."

"No! Anything but that." John cried, dropping on to his knees and mockingly begging for mercy.

The room echoed with their laughter.

"Yow, that hurt!" The wince of pain on John's face, as he tried to get up again, showed his ankle had paid him back for forgetting its fragile state.

"And I thought you were putting it on," I taunted.

"If only."

Just as suddenly as the conversation had turned to murder, so it just as quickly changed to something else. Glasses were recharged, and with the same gusto and hilarity, they resolved another earth-shattering problem.

The evening passed in a twinkling of an eye, and midnight arrived. As if on cue, various members of the group started to make moves towards their bunks. Five or ten minutes later, the cabin was empty.

Chapter 3

Next morning, the blue June sky was almost clear, and the 'normal' stiff breeze was vigorously propelling along the few clouds that still remained from yesterday's storm. The crew of the tug were in the process of lowering a small inflatable dinghy into the almost circular bay. This was being done in a meticulous, slow, and genteel manner because several of the crew members had a distinct fragile feeling.

After the launching had eventually been completed, the two least hungover members of the crew, Phil and Josh, together with Jim and me, climbed into the boat. Phil and Josh rowed Jim and myself over towards the jetty in silence. Noticing that Jim sported a pair of sunglasses, which I had never seen before, I had a sudden urge to make a comment, but then thought it may be better if I ignored them, as I wasn't feeling that robust either myself.

After alighting at the jetty, we left the two crewmembers sitting in the boat and started walking along the rough concrete road that sloped upwards towards the largest building on the island, some half-mile distance.

The largest building consisted of a two-story construction, which also made it the tallest building on the island. Although not located at the geographic centre, it was unmistakably the focal point on the island. Its ground floor housed the generator, workshop, medical treatment area, an administration office, and several other storage areas. The first floor consisted mainly of accommodation, and finally on the flat roof was a makeshift control tower for the airfield.

Radiating from the concrete road that circumvented the central building were four roads, each with ten single-story buildings equally spaced along each side, giving eighty buildings on the island in total. They were constructed from concrete blocks with low-pitched wooden roofs. Just below the eves were a row of long, thin windows high up in the walls, designed to let light in rather than for seeing out, not that there was anything to see if you could see through them. A closer inspection of the structures would have revealed that they had a rough, unfinished appearance on the outside, it wasn't that they were 'jerry-built' just that they had been built in a hurry. A system of gantries carried power cables, drinking water and hot water for heating, and all the other services that were connected between the buildings. Each group terminated or commenced, depending on your point of view, at the central building. The road leading from the jetty, which Jim and I were now walking along, was named 'North Road'. It was named 'North Road' simply because it pointed approximately north.

Directly opposite, on the other side of the central building, was 'South Road'; the two others were called, rather imaginatively, 'East Road' and 'West Road'. East and West Road stopped at the end of their building lines; South Road, however, continued beyond the end of its buildings, onto to the island's small airstrip. This consisted of a short concrete runway, which was only suitable for 'Hercules' type transport aircraft or similar rugged, short take-off and landing aircraft capable of the long flight from the nearest refuelling stop. Dotted around the airstrip were a series of associated storage structures for storing emergency aircraft fuel, plus food, bulk stores, heating oil, and other commodities required to keep the island complex self-sufficient. Also stored along the runway were a quantity of yellow plastic coffins, with their lids, and strips of pig iron. The rest of the island looked windswept and treeless, except for a few stunted bushes that thought they might become trees one day.

The island seemed deserted, apart from me, Jim McNally, and the two other seamen, Phil and Josh, waiting in the dinghy that had brought us ashore. This island was certainly no holiday resort!

As they approached the building, Jim headed for the external door to the administration office, whilst I went up the external stairs into the accommodation area on the first floor.

Inside the scruffy administration office, Doctor Mike Elliot sat at its battered desk, engrossed with typing notes into a computer. The desk was situated against the wall next to the outside door. A decrepit old armchair stood on the other side of the external door. Various racks of shelving, two filing cabinets, and four old plastic chairs clustered around a battered wooden table made up the rest of the room's amenities. Six mugs in assorted conditions of cleanliness stood on the table with their attendant electric kettle and tins of coffee, sugar, and dried milk. The computer Mike was intently bashing away at looked tired, just as the rest of the office did its beige plastic had become discoloured to some indescribable shade of dirty grey. Years of accumulated sweat and filth covered the keyboard, except, that is, for a small round area of shiny plastic in the centre of each keypad, kept clear of grime by the continual pounding of various users' fingers. Jammed in the corner of the room on the end of the desk was a fax machine. Stacks of files were precariously balanced on every available bit of shelf space.

Suddenly the calm of the office was shattered as the external door of the office crashed open and smashed against the end of Mike Elliot's desk. Mike recoiled in his seat and spun round. A split second later, Jim entered, although not quite as dramatically as the door had opened.

"Sorry. The wind snatched the door out of my hand," Jim apologised whilst he closed the door. Blasts of cold wind chilled the whole office as they were funnelled around the room by the closing door.

"You scared the living daylights out of me," retorted Mike.

"That's another two gone for their sea cruise," continued Jim in a flat, unemotional voice, ignoring Mike's cries of distress.

"Thanks," replied Mike.

He lent back in the old typist chair he was sitting on to regain his composure.

"I'll send the appropriate paperwork to London," Mike said this, just as I entered through the internal door at the other end of the office, opposite the one where Jim stood, having come back down from the accommodation area via the internal stairs.

"You're not upsetting Mike, are you Jim?" I taunted, leaning forward into the office by holding onto the top of the doorframe.

Jim nodded in acknowledgement and added, "I seem to have scared him half to death simply by coming through the door."

"It wasn't your coming in that was the problem; it was how you came in that nearly gave me a heart attack."

"At least, there would have been a doctor on hand," I pointed out.

"O very droll."

At that point, the phone rang. Mike lifted the receiver and listened for a few seconds.

"I'll be along in a bit," Mike replied and replaced the receiver.

Swinging his chair round towards Paul, Mike then added, "Roger Wilson in E9 has just collapsed again. Will you go and help the others get him into bed?"

Mike paused, and there was a brief moment of silence as he turned back round to continue typing his notes into the computer.

Then he continued, "I'll be along shortly to take a look at him when I've finished here. Will that be okay?" "I think so," replied Paul.

At this point, Jim turned and started moving back towards the external door.

"You know where to find me," Jim called over his shoulder as he opened the door to leave.

I suddenly had a mischievous thought.

"Want to give us a hand, Jim?" I called after him with a smile.

The reply was exactly as I expected.

"Not bloody likely! It's bad enough having to touch them when they're sealed up in those plastic boxes." Jim's voice was gruff, but there was just a hint of fear in it. However, the rapid closing of the external door prevented any further discussion in that direction.

Pulling myself back into the passage outside the administration office, I closed the door and walked down towards the outside door on the East Side.

Once outside, I headed along East Road until I came to the building with E9 on the door.

Just inside the entrance door were a row of lockers and another door leading into the interior. I opened the locker with my name on it. Hanging inside was a white boiler suit, with a pair of green rubber surgical boots standing at the bottom, and a full-face protection visor located on the top shelf. I retrieved the items and put them on. I took a pair of disposable surgical gloves from one of the boxes next to the internal door and a disposable plastic apron from the other. Turning towards the inner door, I pulled the gloves up to my elbows, over the sleeves of the boiler suite, and tied the apron on. After which I typed in the door's security code into the keypad on the wall next to the door, opened it, and entered the inner part of the building.

There was a short passage leading into the main part of the building, the passage had doors on either side of it, giving access to the toilet facilities. Most of the main part was taken up by two rows of beds, five on each side of the central aisle. An area that doubled as a day room and dining area was located at the far end. The harshness of the overhead fluorescent lights intensified its cold, dispassionate atmosphere.

The two other orderlies were dressed exactly the same as me, with the exception of differing names on the breast pockets of their boiler suits. They were engaged in the process of getting Roger Wilson into one of the beds. Roger had extreme muscle wastage and looked all but dead. Several of the more mobile inmates were standing around watching. As we finished getting Roger into bed, Mike, dressed in his protective gear, came through the door and walked towards us.

He bent over Roger and started examining him. "Any blood or other fluids?" He asked over his shoulder.

"No, not that I can see, and I couldn't see any cuts either. As far as I can make out, he just collapsed onto the open floor," I replied.

"Just the same, give the area a going over with decontaminating fluid. I don't want any of you getting infected and returning in a few years on one of these beds, especially you, Paul, as you're on next week's flight out of here. By the way, the DoH in London has confirmed that Julian West, in S10, has got the new HIV IV strain of the virus. I reckon he'll be going on his sea cruise in about four weeks or so."

"Wasn't he the one who came in on that special flight last week?"

"Yep. I suppose being an ex-minister does give you some contacts to get a cushy flight out here. But it didn't stop him from catching AIDS."

Leaving Mike to finish his examination of Roger, I and the other two orderlies mopped over the floor and left.

The rest of the week passed without incident, apart from Roger Wilson dying, although that was hardly an unusual event on the island. However, it did come rather sooner than expected. I remember helping to get his body into the plastic coffin and transport it down to the jetty for Jim McNally to take on a sea cruise.

On the island, we used coffins made from a single piece of plastic, and the lids were glued on with a solvent, which ensured the body was completely sealed in. These plastic coffins provided better protection from the various body fluids that tended to leak out after death than body bags or coffins made from more conventional materials, especially for those handling the bodies. Two sticks of pig iron were also placed in the coffins to ensure they went straight to the bottom of the ocean and stayed there. Once the coffins were in the sea, the plastic they were made from first became porous and soft, allowing the pressure of the water to crush it flat without bursting and let the salt water slowly seep into the coffin. Thus, facilitating the decomposition of the body and neutralisation of whatever infectious material was left, after which the coffin itself would slowly disintegrate.

Midday Tuesday saw the arrival of the weekly flight up at the airstrip. By the time Mike and I, plus a small group of orderlies, had walked up to the airstrip, food, medical supplies, and a pile of plastic coffins had been unloaded from the Hercules Transport plane. They huddled closely around me, shouting to be heard above the noise of the plane's engines.

"Thanks for five years of your life, Paul. There's nothing like a spell as an ancillary in one of these AIDS colonies to give the rest of your life brilliance and sparkle. I hope you get your degree and things work out for you."

"Thanks Mike. Perhaps, one day, they'll close these places, and you will be able to work in a real hospital. If I had anything to do with it, I'd close them tomorrow."

"Perhaps one day! I don't think I'll hold my breath though."

After a last shaking of hands and embraces, I boarded the plane. The small group moved a short distance away from the plane and watched it trundle down the short runway and eventually heave itself into the sky.

Chapter 4

It was four years, almost to the day, since I had left the Atlantic Island and started working on my degree. Now, having graduated and subsequently determined in myself to try and get some kind of paid employment. With that intent, I had walked from my flat, which is located near Waterloo Railway Station, up to Victoria Street, London, SW1; then I progressed along it until I had located the Department of Health building, which I tentatively entered.

"Whilst I had been on the island, my blond hair had become almost white and was always being blown into a tangled mat during my walks up from the jetty or down from the airfield, or even just going between the buildings. It was the kind of hair that was always unruly and would never look neat, whatever I did with it. But I thought its lightness contrasted very nicely with my outdoor complexion and concentrated the intensity of my grey eyes. Unfortunately, during the time I had spent at university, I had now become urbanised. I had managed, with the help of hair gel, to make my hair acceptably tidy, my outdoor complexion had now faded to a pale reflection of its former self, along with the dwindled intensity of my eyes. I also noted that I would have also gained a few kilogrammes around the middle, if it had not been for the frugality associated with the lifestyle of being a student."

"I had dressed in my best dark suit, white shirt, and tie. Although, in reality, it was the only suit I possessed, and the white shirt and tie had been purchased especially for the interview. I had hoped to blend unobtrusively with the rest of London's business community."

"Having entered the foyer of the Department of Health's building, I noticed it had an Art Deco theme to its decoration, whether this was by design or accident, I didn't have the expertise to tell. There was a vast area of polished marble floors. Along each side were a series of dark, heavy wooden doors leading off," Paul assumed, "into various offices. Clustered outside each of the doors was a small group of plastic chairs, which made what looked like a waiting area, associated with each of the doors."

A semi-circular reception desk in polished mahogany dominated the centre of the wall, which was opposite the main entrance door through which I had just entered. On each side of the reception desk, there were entrances to corridors, which lead off into the bowels of the building. Above the reception desk, but not over it, a balcony ran the full width of the foyer with a door at each end, leading off to what looked like further corridors. Mounted in the centre of the balcony's balustrade was a large ornate clock.

As I walked through the foyer towards the desk. One of the receptionists watched me approach.

"Good morning. I'm Paul Enfield and I have an appointment for an interview this morning. I put my best smile on for the receptionist when I spoke to her."

She smiled back at me, but somehow the smile didn't seem to have any conviction behind it.

After consulting a series of lists in front of her on the desk, she replied in a disinterested voice, "Yes, you are expected. Please could you wait over there next to door number four and someone from personnel will call you in, in due course?"

"Thanks."

I walked over towards the interview waiting area, which was located on the right-hand side of the foyer about halfway down. I remember noting to myself that the receptionist sounded as if she would really like to be somewhere else. The waiting area consisted of two rows of plastic chairs facing each other on either side of the office door. At the top of the door was a small brass number four.

Between the two rows of chairs was a small table with a scattering of out-of-date magazines on it.

There were three vacant seats left in the waiting area for door number four I chose one of the two empty ones in the centre of the left-hand row and settled into it, making myself as comfortable as the hard plastic chair would allow. As I looked around the foyer, "I found it strange how an organisation that could spend so much money in creating such a grand reception area could then destroy the whole image with fifty or so cheap plastic chairs."

After a few moments, I allowed my eyes to scan the other eleven individuals, whom I supposed at the time were also graduate interviewees. However, I noted they looked considerably younger than my twenty-seven years.

Apart from exchanging the occasional twitchy smile in acknowledgement when various pairs of eyes inadvertently locked with each other, we all sat in nervous silence. The time certainly dragged as we waited to be called in turn for our interrogation by the interview board.

"Mr Paul Enfield Please." Came a voice from the doorway.

I stood up and turned towards the voice.

Several times before, I had heard the command and turned in my seat, to see the source of the voice when other members of the group had been called. However, this time, the sound of my name being called caused me to focus more intently on the source of the voice.

"I saw a woman of medium height with a pale, thin, bony complexion standing in the open office doorway. In her hand, she held a clipboard with what Paul assumed was a list of their names. She wore a dark suit, although he couldn't make out whether it was a dark navy blue or black in the subdued lighting of the waiting area. Her age was equally difficult to pinpoint; he guessed forty, but the back of his mind suggested another five years or so on top." I could feel the eyes of the remaining interviewees watching me walk towards the doorway, just as he himself had watched the earlier ones. As he reached the door, she stood aside in order to allow him to enter the room first.

"Please take a seat in that chair, Mr Enfield," she said, indicating the wooden upright chair situated at the centre of the room.

After closing the door, she joined the other two interviewers behind a long table situated at the far end of the room. The room seemed relatively large, considering the amount of furniture it contained, and was decorated in various drab shades of light brown and magnolia. Paul's chair, the long table, and the chairs occupied by the three interviewers behind it were the only items in the room. It had a depressing, intimidating atmosphere and instantly reminded him of the interrogation scenes depicted in the old war films he had watched from time to time. For a split second, my mind wandered, imagining the three interviewers in German uniform.

"Thank you for attending this interview, Dr Enfield. Please, relax, and make yourself comfortable. My name is Miss Jasmine Arkwright, and I am head of personnel."

Although not loud, Jasmine's voice had a penetrating quality, which seemed to jar deep inside Paul's brain, preventing it from being ignored. It certainly refocused my mind from the German uniforms and back to the current reality.

"Hallo," I replied.

"This is Dr Preston, our occupational psychiatrist."

"Hallo."

"And this is head of security, Major Smithson."

"Hallo."

I acknowledged each one of them in turn, in a mild, pleasant voice.

Jasmine continued, "First, I would like you to satisfy my curiosity regarding the period between you leaving school and starting university. According to your CV, you volunteered as a medical ancillary for a period of five years. I know it's quite common for students to take a gap year, so I checked with your university. They said you specifically asked for a five-year gap before taking up your place, so it wasn't because you failed to get a university place. Perhaps you would enlighten us as to the reasons for taking so much time out from your studies."

"Whilst I was studying my A-levels at school, our careers master suggested, in fact recommended, we look at some of the more unusual aspects of the standard career choices. I was interested in health care at the time, so with the help of the master, I wrote to several agencies, who gave me some contacts. One of these contacts made an interesting offer that I liked the sound of.

"Consequently, I spent those five years, between leaving school and starting university, looking after AIDS sufferers as a student orderly at…"

"Have you signed the Official Secrets Act?" Major Smithson's voice suddenly interjected, interrupting Paul's descriptive flow.

"Yes," I replied, rather surprised at being cut short so impolitely.

Dr Preston, sensing Paul had been unsettled by Major Smithson's interruption, also cut in.

"The positions we are interviewing for today don't actually have anything to do with patients. You do know that, didn't Mr Enfield?" Dr Preston informed Paul in a demining tone of voice.

Paul paused for a few seconds to regain his composure before answering.

Addressing Dr Preston, Paul continued, "Yes, I was fully aware of that fact. My current career aspirations do not lay in the direction of direct patient care. My five years of experience in that field have fully convinced me of that."

As he started to answer Dr Preston's question, out of the corner of his eye, Paul noticed Major Smithson lean over and whisper something in Miss Arkwright's ear.

"Quite so," again Major Smithson's interrupted, cutting Dr Preston short this time. "Have you ever belonged to a left-wing political party or held strong views on any particular aspect of government? Like freedom of information, for instance."

I suddenly and instinctively came to the conclusion that Major Smithson was just a pompously rude ex-Guard's dropout. As a consequence of this, I decided that the kind of answer I would give to Smithson's questions would be short and curt, just short of being contemptuous.

"No," I replied.

"I just wanted to make sure you are aware of the positions being considered here today, Mr Enfield," Dr Preston explained, trying to regain some kind of psychological advantage over Paul, but the look in Paul's eyes made him realise the Major's intimidating attitude would have no further impact.

"Thank you for explaining what you were involved in during that five-year period, Mr Enfield I don't think there is any further reason to dwell on that point anymore," said Miss Arkwright. She then suddenly altered the direction of the interview towards more mundane things. "Would you please tell us how you see your career developing in the future and why you feel that working for the Department of Health would help you achieve those goals?" she asked.

"The interview continued unremarkably for a further thirty-five minutes. After the interview had finished, I left the building and went out onto Victoria Street."

"Strangely, Major Smithson's interruption bothered me, but I couldn't put my finger on the reason why. Something about it was not cognitively sitting right in my brain.

However, after walking for about ten minutes, mulling the incident over inside my head, I was still unable to discern what had given cause for my apprehension. Eventually, I decided to put it out of my mind; after all, the outcome of the interview was now out of my influence."

It was exactly seven days later, when I received a letter from the Department of Health. Which, much to my astonishment, stated that my interview had been successful and I was being offered a position as a research assistant. This was even more surprising, when I reflected on how insolent my attitude could have been interpreted during the opening stages of the interview. Along with the memories of the interview, came my niggling concern about Major Smithson's attitude and his involvement in the cross examination.

"For no specific reason, I suddenly contemplated that perhaps Major Smithson exhibited the same insolence towards all the interviewees. Consequently, the other two members of the interview board had totally ignored any upset he caused the particular interviewee."

"Despite those thoughts, I still suspected something had happened or had been said at that interview to make my subconscious unhappy with Major Smithson's conduct," Paul reasoned with himself. "Resulting in giving me a strange gut-feeling, and the only way I am going to get at the bottom of it, is to take up this new position."

He glanced at the letter again; it stated he was to report at the Victoria Street entrance of the Department of Health on the first Monday of the next month.

Chapter 5

It was five minutes to nine, when, amidst all the normal Monday morning rush hour crowd, I again entered through the main doors of the Department of Health building, in Victoria Street, and walked through the foyer, towards the reception desk.

Paul had to wait five or so minutes whilst the receptionist behind the desk dealt with someone else.

"Can I help you, sir?" the receptionist asked after she had finished dealing with her previous person.

"Good Morning. My name's Paul Enfield, and I have been instructed to come here to start work this morning."

The receptionist consulted a list, and after a few moments, she replied in the same preoccupied voice she had used on his initial visit to attend his interview.

"Yes, you are expected; would you please wait over there with the others, Mr Enfield? Miss Arkwright, head of personnel, will be out and call you through at nine o'clock." She said, pointing to where three other people were sitting, in a row of six plastic chairs, situated against the left-hand wall of the foyer.

I moved over to where they were sitting and selected one of the empty plastic chairs. As I approached the row of chairs,

I recognised the other three occupants from the day of my interview. I nodded in acknowledgement and exchanged a polite, "Good morning."

The hands on the clock, above the reception desk, eventually clicked round to exactly nine o'clock.

Instantly, as if she had been waiting just out of sight, for the hands of the clock to move round to nine o'clock, Miss Jasmine Arkwright came out of the left-hand corridor, located besides the reception desk, and walked over to where the four of them were seating.

"Good morning. It's nice to see you're all here, on time. First, I'll be taking you to the security office to get your passes made up, then to the personnel department for you to sign various forms and other relative paperwork. Then someone will give you a tour of the building, pointing out the go and no-go areas and other points of interest relative to your particular jobs—please follow me," announced Miss Jasmine Arkwright.

Having introduced herself with those few words, Jasmine turned and strode purposefully from the foyer and down the long corridor from which she had just emerged.

The four new starters all scrambled to their feet and hurriedly followed after her. It took about five minutes for the little procession to reach the security office. Its glass door and the panels facing the corridor had been glazed in frosted glass. Jasmine knocked on the door and entered, followed by Paul and the other three new starters.

"This is Major Smithson; head of security; you will probably remember him from your interviews."

"Good morning," Major Smithson's voice sounded more pompous than it had at the interview.

"I guessed that sometime in the past, he had been retired from one of the Guard's regiments; however, he could just as easily have been a dropout, which is what I thought at my interview," Paul contemplated to himself.

Once again, the nagging recollections of Smithson's attitude during my interview raised its ugly head, and I again wondered what had happened or been said, which his subconscious mind had objected to.

After a series of forms had been signed, they took turns having their photograph taken and the appropriate security passes, depending on which department they were going to be assigned to, made up by Major Smithson.

"Mr Enfield, please do not smile at the camera in the future. It's not a beauty contest," commented Jasmine, with a pained voice, as she checked the passes.

From the security office, they all followed Jasmine to the personnel office, signed more forms, and were given a New-Employee Starter's Pack, which contained a map of the building, fire evacuation instructions, an employee's handbook, and other similar documents.

Having eventually completed all the necessary formalities, I was introduced to an Office Junior named Sue. Jasmine instructed her to show me to the area where I would be working. However, it was obvious from her attitude that she had been allocated this task many times before and now viewed it as a repugnant chore, which she would try to avoid if at all possible.

The two of them left the personnel office, and she led the way up to the first floor.

"That's the copying room," droned Sue's bored voice as she waved an arm in the general direction of a nondescript door.

"Is everyone who works in this place bored?" I inquired.

"There are those that are bored and those that are boring; you'll have to work out who's which for yourself. By the way, that's the Gent's Loo over there."

Another general wave as they passed a door, which displayed a small plastic man on it.

"That's the Ladies Loo, the door with the small plastic woman on it. You won't need to know that, though."

Another general wave, after which she turned and grinned at me.

"Thank you. I suppose I should be pleased that I got a nice smile from you. Anyway, you never know, I might find a use for it."

Sue gave me a very strange, slightly puzzled, sideways look.

"This is the General Archiving Office."

At this point, the corridor had opened out into an open-plan office area, with fifteen or so desks arranged in small groups throughout the area. Several of the computer operators looked up as we walked past and acknowledged Sue the others took no notice.

Sue continued with another wave, "The old dragon, who's in charge of this department, sits at that desk in the far corner, but she's never there, as you can see."

The two of them had now reached the other end of the open-plan area. and entered another corridor.

"This is your office, the one with Mr Pratt on the door. Best of luck; you'll need it. No one ever works for him very long. He acts like his name—a Pratt!"

We continued further along the corridor, until they came to a flight of stairs, which led up to the next floor.

"The archive and general library are on the next floor up; there is also another set of toilets and a copier up there," Sue informed me with the usual wave.

"Not in the same room, I hope," I remarked, hoping to elucidate a note of humour from Sue.

"O' very funny. Anyway, this is where I leave you. I hope you cope with working for David Pratt. I'll see you around Paul."

"Thanks Sue."

I walked back down the corridor, wondering what I was going to find, until coming to Mr Pratt's office. Paul knocked on the door and entered.

Standing in the doorway, I surveyed what I thought was an empty office. It contained two desks; each one had a computer terminal on it, one immaculately tidy and the other looked like a wastepaper bin had been emptied over it. David Pratt, Paul's supervisor, was aged about fifty-four with a skeletal face; his grey hair was slicked back, and he wore a black pinstriped suit. He happened to be standing behind the door—hidden from Paul—as I opened it. Consequently, when he started to talk, it came as quite a surprise.

"Who are you, and what do you want?" David Pratt demanded.

"O' good morning. My name is Paul Enfield, and I have been told I'll be starting work here this morning."

"Mine's the clear desk! Yours is the one with the rubbish on it; you'd better clear it up," Pratt addressed Paul with a contemptuous tone.

"Thank you," replied Paul. Then added under his breath, "Now I know what Sue meant."

"What was that?" snapped Pratt.

"O' nothing, I was thinking out loud."

"Don't even think about starting to get impudent! I'll have you out on the street, as quick as that, if you're not careful."

I decided not to pick a verbal fight with him this early in our acquaintance. Consequently, I bit my tongue and placed all the documents and forms I had collected from the security office and personnel at one end of my desk, and I started to clear the rubbish away and put it in the waste paper bin.

"I suppose I'd better give you time to read all that junk before you start work," Pratt condescended, with a sarcastic note in his voice.

"Thank you very much," Paul replied, but added silently, "you might think you have the upper hand; however, I shall win the war!"

Chapter 6

Up on the second floor, in one of the small offices used for filing. Miss Caroline Aston was bending over and rummaging in one of the filling cabinet's lower drawers, looking for some older documents she had been tasked with finding. She had short red hair, milky white skin, and a round face, covered in freckles. As the office was located in a quiet area of the building, so as not to be isolated and hidden from those passing by, she had propped the office door open with a fire extinguisher.

Picking a moment when the outside corridor was empty, Mr Blackstone, Caroline's Head of Section, lifted the extinguisher away from the door and went into the room behind her, allowing the door to close quietly behind him so that anybody passing wouldn't notice what was going on in the office. Engrossed in her search, Mr Blackstone's presence went unnoticed by Caroline. He crept up behind her. Suddenly he slid his hand up her skirt, between her legs, and grabbed her crotch.

Caroline spun round. Swiped Blackstone across the face with the back of her hand and headed for the door.

Rubbing his face, Blackstone shouted after her, "I'll get you fired for that!"

But before he had time to say or do anything else, Caroline had shot out of the office and slamming the door behind her. She raced down to the personnel office and charged in.

Jasmine Arkwright was seated at the desk of her inner office with its door open when Caroline arrived in the outer office.

"Miss Aston, please come in and sit down. How can I help you? You seem to be in quite a state."

Before she had reached the chair in Jasmine's office, Caroline franticly started recounting her encounter a few seconds earlier. "It's Mr Blackstone. He's just put his hand up my skirt whilst I was in the filling room. I had propped the door open with a fire extinguisher. Whilst I was looking in the filing cabinet, he removed the extinguisher and quietly closed the door, crept up behind me, and then put his hand up my skirt and grabbed my private parts."

"Yes, yes. I have just had a phone call from Mr Blackstone to that effect. However, he said it was you who did the touching, and when he protested, you hit him to make it look like it was his fault."

"I tell you he grabbed my crotch from behind—that's why I hit him. He never said a word before I hit him, so that's a lie."

"Caroline, we've been down this road before, haven't we? There was that occasion with Mr Wilson."

Caroline's voice raised itself an octave, "Are you calling me a liar? I'm beginning to think; you think I do it on purpose. Blackstone said he would get me the sack, the pervert!"

"Let's try and resolve this without hysterics, can we. Sit down. When did he say that?"

Caroline sank into a chair.

"After I hit him and before I got out the door. I'd rather leave than work with that depraved monster again. This place seems to be full of perverts. You believe his story—don't you—you believe that I gave him the come on."

"Caroline, please try and calm down. Look, you're not going to get the sack. I'll arrange for you to be transferred to an open-plan office with a female head of department, which will hopefully remove or at least reduce the chances of you becoming cornered."

On hearing Jasmine Arkwright's reassurance, Caroline sat back in her chair and visibly relaxed.

Jasmine continued, "I know you don't flirt with them or give them any kind of come on, because I made a point of having you watch to ascertain who was telling me the truth about these events you get involved in."

Caroline's face turned scarlet as Jasmine continued, dreading what's going to be said next.

"You just seem to make men want to attack you. It's not what you do, or say, it just happens. I suppose it must be your body chemistry. I fully believe that you don't mean, or want to cause problems, they just seem to come looking for you. I suppose it's a bit like a moth and the way they're attracted to the flame of a candle and then get themselves burnt. Look, it's Thursday today, and you've had a rather traumatic experience. I want you to have the rest of today and tomorrow off, and I'll get things organised for a new start on Monday morning. However, I do not want you to talk to anyone about this, because I need to investigate Mr Blackstone a bit further. Unlike Mr Wilson, there have been rumours that Mr Blackstone has been involved in similar events of this kind before, but no one has been willing to come forward and substantiate them. I realise that the other women he attacked may have believed Mr Blackstone's threat that he could get them sacked and consequently didn't report the event."

"You mean I've done you a favour?"

"I wouldn't quite go as far as saying that, but it could be helpful. Do you want me to come with you and get your things from your workstation, before you go home? I think it will help avoid any unpleasant encounters with Mr Blackstone."

"Yes, please, thank you."

The pair of them walked to the area where Caroline's workstation was located. In the distance, Caroline noticed Mr Blackstone sitting at his desk, who, as soon as he noticed Caroline heading for her workstation, leapt out of his chair and started to head towards her. However, as soon as he noticed Jasmine accompanying her, decided to wheel round and disappear.

Chapter 7

On Monday morning of the following week, as Paul walked through the foyer, he involuntary glanced up at the clock and noted it was showing eight fifty. A few moments later, he passed through the open-plan area towards David Pratt's office. As he is about to enter the office, he turns and sees that Jasmine had brought a redheaded girl in and was introducing her to the departmental supervisor.

Paul smiled and muttered to himself, "She must be Sue's 'Old Dragon'. Well, she's in today."

Unfortunately, without Paul being aware of it, Pratt had come along the corridor from the opposite direction and was now close enough to hear Paul's muttered comment.

"What's that supposed to mean?" Pratt demanded, "Get in that office."

Paul, momentarily stunned, entered first and sat down at his desk. Pratt followed him in, slammed the door, and stood opposite him on the other side of Paul's desk. Glaring down at Paul, seated opposite, Pratt tried to intimidate him. However, instead of cowering before this attempted intimidation, Paul looked him straight in the eyes with a genteel smile and a benign look on his face. Having been emotionally short-circuited, Pratt suddenly went round and sat down at his own desk. He sat there, opening and closing his mouth for some time, without any sound coming out.

Pratt, still with a demanding attitude, broke the silence that had lasted for several minutes.

"I want to know what all this Sue Dragon business is about."

"It's a private matter, and I'm not going to tell you," still with the benign look on his face.

Pratt had never had to deal with someone who was not frightened of him. Consequently, he was now struggling to achieve a normal level of communication. Paul sat in silence, watching, whilst Pratt struggled with the unknown.

After several aborted attempts, Pratt continued, "I saw you looking at that girl out there."

"Yes, that's right."

"I don't like that sort of thing in my department."

"What sort of thing is that?"

"I'm warning you. One of my colleagues has been removed from the post of head of department, and now another is under investigation. All because she accused them of attacking her."

"Did they?"

"What?" replied Pratt, rather bewildered at the way the conversation was going.

"Did your friends attack her?"

"No, of course they didn't. They're respectable married men and wouldn't do such a thing, and anyway, I know her type!"

Paul, knowing he now had the upper hand, kept his voice quiet and calm.

"What type is that?"

Pratt's voice now began to indicate he was starting to lose control completely.

"Sex maniac! That's her type. She tried to get them to have sex with her. When they refused, she frames them out of vengeance."

"You have evidence for this charge?"

"I…do…not…need…it. I…know…the…type!" replied Pratt through clenched teeth.

"Have you spoken to personnel about this; it may help your friends?"

The strain of Paul interrogating him, rather than the other way round, proved too much for Pratt. He crashed his chair back against the wall and stormed out of the office. Paul grinned as the door slammed and leant back in his chair.

After a few moments of savouring his victory, Paul noticed a copy of the report, 'Current Trends in Hospital Admissions', he had produced earlier in the week, lying on Pratt's desk.

He went round and started to read it; immediately it was obvious to him that some of the data, wording, and conclusions had been changed. Going back to his desk, he switches on his computer and starts to check his original version of the report against Pratt's modified version.

"What's Pratt up to?" he said out loud to himself, "changing my report. These changes make it look as if the current trend in hospital admissions is on the decrease, whereas the original data shows it's increasing. Why has he changed it?"

Reaching over, Paul replaced the report back on Pratt's desk. At the same instant, Pratt stormed back into the office.

"What are you doing on my desk?" The earlier hysteria in his voice had gone.

"Reading my report. Why have you changed it?"

"Mind your own business. Don't poke your snout in where it's not supposed to be."

"That report has got my name on it, so that makes it my business."

"No, it doesn't; as your superior, I can do what I like with your reports. Just get on with what you're given and stop trying to cause trouble."

After a few moments of strained silence, Paul got up and left the office.

As the door closed, Pratt picked up the phone and dialled security, "Major Smithson, please. Hallo Major, this is David Pratt. I think we may have a potential problem with Paul Enfield. Can you arrange for his computer access to be restricted to the public domain only? Thanks."

Paul stands at the end of the corridor leading from Pratt's office into the general archive office area. The head of the department, who Paul only knew as Sue's Dragon, sees him and comes over to him without being noticed.

"Can I help you?" she asks.

"O', Hallo, your Sue's D…"

Paul managed to stop himself from saying Dragon but looked extremely embarrassed as a result. Sue's Dragon exploded with laughter.

"You were shown round this area by Sue, weren't you?"

"Yes, why?"

"She's my daughter, and our family name is Dragon. I bet she didn't tell you that."

"No, she didn't. Wait till I see her again," replied Paul rather sheepishly.

"Don't worry about it. It's a joke that we have between us. She gets the pleasure of calling me an old dragon, and I get the pleasure of seeing people's faces when I tell them the truth, and yours was a picture. Anyway, how can I help you?"

"I don't know what your feelings are towards Mr Pratt, but I think it would be better for both him and me if I found a place to work outside his office."

"So, you're the poor so and so who got lumbered with that position; you have my deepest sympathy. Watch out for yourself; with him, he's a nasty bit of work. Anyway, that computer in the far corner is not allocated to anyone, and it's fairly secluded, so you could use that if you want to."

They moved over to where the computer was located, in the corner of the General Archiving Office that was furthest from Pratt's office. The intervening desks and computers between Pratt's office and the corner where the computer was located, although not hiding him, would make Paul reasonably inconspicuous to Pratt in the event that he came out of his office.

"All the computers in this building are the same, so you can login as you would on the one in your office. Anything else?"

"No, I don't think so," replied Paul. "Thanks for your help."

"No problem, just ask if there is anything contrary to what Sue probably told you, I'm usually around."

Sue's Dragon watches whilst Paul logs into the computer and finds he is unable to access his last report.

"That's strange, I was looking at that report less than half hour ago. Are you sure that this computer has the same access level?"

"Yes, I know it has. But I know what's happened; you've had your access clearance restricted to the public data domain only. Have you upset Pratt already?"

"You'd have a job not to."

"I bet he's had your security clearance lowered out of spite. Pratt and Smithson have become very cooperative and close over the last few years, which, thinking about it, is interesting because they never used to be. I transgress, will it affect your work?"

"I'm not sure; I suppose that will depend on the next project he gives me. I suppose it's time I went and found out what it is. By the way, what should I call you?"

"How about Sue's Dragon?" The laughing reply came over her shoulder as she walked away.

Mr Pratt was sitting at his desk working as Paul came into the office.

"The outline of your next project is on your desk. Its title is 'The Decreasing Incidents of Incurable Diseases'."

"Why have you had my computer access restricted?"

"Nothing to do with me. Security is Major Smithson's department. You'll have to take it up with him. He's probably discovered you're some kind of activist or left-wing troublemaker. Anyway, you've got all the clearance you need for that project."

"How do you know that when I haven't told you what my new clearance is?"

"The lowest clearance is good enough for what's needed with that simple project."

Paul had detected the note of provocation in his voice but chose not to rise to the bait and let it go without comment.

"Don't make yourself comfortable in that seat; I don't think you will be staying here very long," Pratt sneered. "Your next project is on your desk; just go and get on with it."

Paul was about to comment that it wouldn't matter what he wrote, as Pratt would change it anyway, but chose not to.

Taking the outline of his new project with him, he left Pratt's office and reconciled himself at the new desk, temporarily allocated to him by Sue's Dragon. Sometime later, she walks over to him.

"How's it going?"

"It's much better working out here. However, something is wrong with this data, or should I say the data I'm allowed to see. It just seems to fit the required answers too closely—as if it's been, dare I say, doctored."

"It's well known that Pratt does not hold much by the accuracy of his reports, provided they support the government's current policy, that is. Look; let me log in; no one will know. At least, it'll get you into another data area. Perhaps the data there will be more believable. Unfortunately, I can't help you beyond that." She leans over Paul and logs herself into the system.

"Give me a shout when you log off. Security is automatically notified if anyone is logged into more than one terminal at the same time. I won't log in on mine until you've finished."

Paul smiled at her, "I didn't know that thanks, err…Sue's Dragon."

She smiled and walked away, and Paul starts examining the data at the new security level, which he finds is not much better than the first lot. Deep in thought, he gets up and turns to go over towards Sue's Dragon. As he swings round, he collides with Caroline, who was walking past with a load of data entry slips. She was on her way towards her desk in order to enter them into her computer terminal. However, Paul's collision with Caroline sent the data entry sips flying across the floor. Paul, Caroline, and some others start scrambling around the floor, retrieving the scattered slips.

All of a sudden Paul sees a name on one of the slips he has just picked up and freezes. At this point, Pratt comes out of his office, attracted by the commotion at the other end of the office.

Pratt shouts across the office, "Enfield! What do you think you're up to? Leave that girl alone. Stop trying to get off with her and get up here now."

Paul is now fuming at this false accusation and starts to walk towards Pratt, intent on putting him in the hospital. Sue's Dragon, realising what Paul is about to do to Pratt, rushes over and puts herself between Paul and Pratt.

Putting her face next to his, she insists, "Get out. Go home now; go anywhere but here. He's not worth it!"

"I've had enough! He's going to pay for that," uttered Paul in a raised voice.

"Listen," Sue stated, "if you touch him, he'll win, and that's what he wants you to do. Don't give him the satisfaction of winning."

Paul turns to leave. But says in a stern voice, "I'll find a way of getting back at him."

With that, he leaves the area.

Sue Dragon also turns, but to face Pratt, "You may regret that."

"I don't think so. What's he going to do? Report me for stopping him from touching that girl. No, I don't think he'll do anything," he replied sneeringly.

After leaving the office, Paul, still fuming, started to walk towards his flat. On the way, he called into an off-licence and brought a case of twenty-four beer cans. Continuing on his way, he wandered the long way around, trying to dispel his infuriation. He eventually reached his flat, unlocked the door, and entered his flat. Dumping his jacket on the floor and kicking his shoes into a corner, he threw himself onto sofa, and started drinking the beer at an industrial rate in order to try and drown the anger and frustration that had built up inside him.

An hour or so later, he eventually fell asleep, snoring loudly, surrounded on the floor by a considerable number of empty beer cans.

Chapter 8

It was about nine o'clock of the same evening, when a succession of relentless knocking on the front door ultimately roused Paul out of his drunken stupor. Eventually, Paul managed to open the front door. To his surprise, he finds Caroline standing there.

"Hallo," Caroline said.

"Who are you?" Paul inquired, still a bit incoherent.

"I'm Caroline, the girl you attacked in the office earlier—remember."

"O' yes, I remember. I'm sorry. I've had a few drinks that have gone to my head, and I must have dosed off."

"Are you going to let me in then?"

"I'm sorry. Yes, of course. Please come in."

"Thanks."

Paul had started to become more coherent by now. Suddenly, he noticed the state the room was in.

"Please excuse the clutter. Would you like a drink?"

"Yes, please, if there's some left to have," retorted Caroline.

Paul tried to pick up, but only partly successfully, the scattered empty cans and take them into the kitchen area. He returned with two full ones and handed one to Caroline.

"Look, I'm sorry about this mess and about what happened in the office earlier."

"Actually, it was quite funny, really. It's the first time someone has been accused of attacking me when they hadn't. Usually, they really do try and get off with me. After you left the office, that stupid man, Pratt, came over to me and tried to convince me that it was you who was doing all the grabbing. That was despite the fact that my boss had witnessed what happened, and Pratt hadn't even come out of his office until after we had nearly finished picking up the slips," Caroline recounted, trying hard not to laugh. "Do you believe my account, or Pratt's?"

"At the moment, all I want to do is to put Pratt in a hospital. Who does he think he is? No, I believe your side of the story," Paul confirmed.

"Well, I thought you were about to do just that, i.e., put Pratt into hospital, that is, if my boss hadn't prevented you."

"Good job she did. Anyway, why have you come here?" Paul asked, "More to the point, how did you know where I live?"

Caroline handed him the data entry slip from the office, which had made him freeze.

"I've brought this for you to look at. Why is it so interesting?" Caroline asked, "I've entered hundreds of these things into my computer throughout today. By the way, it's my first day in the archive office."

"Yes, I know. I saw you being introduced this morning. You see the name on this slip, Julian West. Well, he died at least four years ago. Yet this slip says he died last month in Scotland, on a climbing holiday. When I last saw him, he couldn't climb into bed—let alone go climbing mountains. What's going on?" Paul questioned.

"It obviously a different Julian West," replied Caroline.

"I'm not stupid! No chance. Look, the slip's got his National Insurance number on it. I could never forget that sequence of numbers and letters HI 05 04 01 D."

"Why is that number so significant?"

"He was one of the first patients to die of AIDS, which had developed from the HIV IV virus."

"So?"

"Look at it. 'H', 'I', five is 'V' in roman numerals, so that's HIV. The four's obvious, and so is the number one, and the 'D' stands for death," Paul explained.

"It's a bit cryptic. How do you know that's not just a coincidence?" Caroline asked.

"First, you tell me how you found out my address?" Paul insisted.

"It seems that there are secrets in both our pasts. OK. As I came to see you, I suppose I'd better tell you my secret first. By the way, I hope you're not a prude."

"I can assure you, that's one thing I'm not," Paul retorted.

"When I left school at sixteen, I meet a man; well, he seemed like a man to me then, and he was about twenty-two. We had loads of fun together, and the sex was great, so I moved in with him on my eighteenth birthday. After I had moved in with him, I discovered he was a semi-professional computer hacker. He would adjust various company accounts, so an invoice became lost or increased in value, depending on what was required—for consideration, of course. Over the three years I stayed with him, he taught me all the tricks and skills necessary to do computer hacking. Since then, I've developed a few methods of my own, for dealing with the various improved computer security methods and devices that have been developed over the years since, and I have managed to get round all of them.”

“You don’t look old enough to have done all that,” Paul condescended.

“Please! Don’t try that chat-up line with me,” interjected Caroline, with a sharp edge on her voice.

“It’s all right don’t get on your high horse; I’m not patronising you,” Paul retorted.

“Anyway, that’s how I got your address—I just went into personnel’s records and looked. It took about thirty seconds. That’s my secret.” Caroline explained, “Come on then, let’s hear your story,” Caroline demanded.

“After taking my A’ levels, I gained a place at university. I intended to ask if I could take a year off before starting ‘To See the World’. Most students were doing it. However, after getting the university place, I was approached by an agency. They wanted to know if I would like to work in patient care for five years. As I was interested in that sort of thing at that time, I said yes, thinking it would be in a hospital somewhere. However, because I was about to go to university, they said they would fix it for me to have the time off, and they did. In due course, a heap of forms came in the post, which I filled in and sent back. I was taken to have a medical at a private hospital in Peterborough. After the medical, I was taken to an office. The man in the office told me to read a document concerning the Official Secrets Act and sign it. He then told me I would be working on a small island, in the South Atlantic, helping to cure AIDS patients.”

"You mean you might have caught AIDS!" Caroline interjected.

"No. I was only looking after them, that is, until they died anyway," Paul corrected her.

"You're lying! You can catch it by just touching them."

"Don't be stupid! How do you know anything about it anyway?" Paul snapped.

Caroline grabbed her things and headed for the door.

"Don't call me stupid. I'm getting out of here. You've probably given it to me already. You pervert!" Caroline shouted as she slammed the front door. Paul shouted after her, "Come back and don't be so bloody ignorant!"

The last part of Paul's sentence was lost in the slamming of his front door.

After a minute or so silence, he remonstrated to himself, "I suppose I'd better go and find her, in case she really does think she's caught AIDs and tries to top herself. Stupid Cow."

Paul walked through the many interconnecting pedestrian walkways under the southern end of Waterloo Bridge, down the side off the National Theatre on to the riverside and then up the stairs onto the bridge itself.

"This is stupid, as if this is the only place in London where someone would try to kill themselves," he muttered to himself.

Paul was just over three-quarters of the way across the bridge. Suddenly he becomes aware of a car coming up behind him with two wheels on the pavement. Realising the car was heading towards him, Paul sprinted the last fifty or so yards to the gap where the steps lead down to the embankment below. He managed to get into the opening there just before the car did, which by this time was scraping along the bridge's parapet. After passing the gap that Paul had taken refuge in, the car roared down the underpass.

"Heck! What on earth was that driver up to?" Paul exclaimed.

"Paul, is that you?" Asked a voice emanating from under the arch of the bridge.

Paul, still dumbfounded by his near miss, turned and started to descend the steps to investigate where the voice had come from. As he clatters down the steps, he finds Caroline coming up the steps to meet him.

"Caroline! What are you doing here? Don't tell me you were going to jump off the bridge, just because you thought you had AIDS."

"Come on, please do give me some credit; I'm not a suicide case—not yet anyway. Mind you, I did panic back there though. It's that word AIDS—it's like the modern Black Death. Go on then, you can have your gloat; yes, I was stupid. There happy now?"

Chapter 9

They climbed up onto Waterloo Bridge and started walking back towards Paul's flat.

"Look, I promise I've never had or expect to get AIDS," Paul stated, in as reassuring voice as possible.

"It's all right, I believe you," Caroline acquiesced.

"Now here's a really good chat-up line. Do you want to come back to my place, for a nightcap?" Paul said, smiling, I have a spare bedroom.

"Are you taking the proverbial?"

"Just a little. As I don't know where you live, how can I offer to take you home?"

"It's all right, I'll come back to your place."

"Seriously though, I don't want you to end up having another session of the screaming add-dabs."

"No, I promise I won't, doing it the first time made me feel really stupid enough," Caroline confessed.

They both walked across the bridge and through all the interconnecting walkways at the southern end of the Waterloo Bridge and then onto Paul's flat.

"Come in and make yourself comfortable," Paul instructed, whilst he went into the kitchen area and started preparing a drink.

Meanwhile, Caroline removed her coat and flopped on to the sofa.

"Have you been living here long?" Caroline asked.

"Not really. Only about four and a half years; I got it just before I started university. Do you want coffee, or shall we open a bottle of wine?" Came Paul's reply from the kitchen.

"Wine," responded Caroline.

Paul came into the living area.

"One bottle of Château la Plonk," announced Paul as he removed the cork from the wine bottle.

"Do you want to let it breathe?"

"Blow convention, just pour it in a glass," Caroline instructed, "and let's drink it."

Obediently, Paul poured the wine into two glasses and sat on the sofa, next to Caroline.

"Actually, I was quite lucky to get this flat, especially a two-bedroom one. Through a friend, plus being in the right place at the right time. Where are you living?"

"I've got a bedsit in the East End. I saved about a fiver by walking over to the other side of the river before getting a taxi, which is why I was at the northern end of the Waterloo Bridge."

"Did you see the drunken fool in the car, which nearly killed me on the bridge?" Paul queried.

"Not really. All I saw was a fast car, which looked very close to the parapet."

"Close enough to have squashed me against it if I hadn't legged into the gap where you were. He must have wrecked the side of his car, most probably stoned out of his tiny mind."

"How do you know it was him? It might have been she." Caroline mooted controversially.

"Yes, I know. I'll call it an 'It', then I must be right. Although that does raise another question—was he drunk, sorry, 'It', or was it deliberate?"

Caroline started laughing, "Aren't we getting a bit on the paranoiac side?"

"Probably some jealous husband out to kill you because you attacked his wife in the office yesterday."

"You will be telling me next; it was your husband who was driving the car."

"Well, on your performance this afternoon, I'd want a reassessment as to whether it could even be classed as a push, let alone an attack," Caroline replied contemptuously. Anyway, can I please have a sleepover in your spare room, so I don't have to risk being rundown by a wayward car?

Next morning, Caroline was watching Paul, who was sitting on the sofa in his underpants, putting his socks on. She poked him in the side to get his attention.

"Do you always put your socks on first?" Caroline observed.

"Don't do that; it hurts. Yes, I do."

"We're a bit touchy this morning, aren't we?" Paul moved out of Caroline's reach.

"A bit too much beer before the wine. It's made me a bit fragile. Just leave me alone," Paul asserted grumpily.

"You did have a bit of a head start on me. How many did you have before I got here?"

"I can't remember—ten may be twenty or so. I was just trying to drown Pratt in beer. By the way, what if that car did mean to kill me last night?"

"Why, do you think I've got a jealous boyfriend, or something?" queried Caroline.

"No. Of course not. I wasn't thinking like that. What if it's got something to do with this AIDS thing I'm mixed up with?"

"Now who's being paranoid? You'll be saying next it's Pratt trying to eliminate you, for upsetting him," Caroline proclaimed, whilst she was laughing.

"Come on, get yourself organised, else you'll have Sue's Dragon breathing fire on you."

"Who, or what is Sue's Dragon?"

"Don't you know who your boss is?"

"No. I didn't catch her name when we were introduced. What is it?"

"Mrs Dragon. The rest will take too long to explain, but it's a joke between me and her."

"You're having me on?" Caroline declared as she finished getting ready to leave.

"No, I'm not, and I'll prove it when we get to the office. I suppose I've got to face Pratt sooner or later. Come on."

"Are we going by taxi?" Caroline inquired tentatively.

"No, we are going to walk; all though, it will probably be dawdle all the way," Paul insinuated.

Eventually they set off towards Victoria Street.

Chapter 10

After arriving back up on the floor where they worked, Paul and Caroline walked over towards Sue's Dragon, who was sitting at her desk, and stood next to her at the desk. However, Caroline's face showed that she was totally unconvinced that this pending confrontation would prove anything.

"Hello, Sue's Dragon. You know Caroline, of course," Paul said, smiling.

Sue's Dragon looked up at both of them, sensing that there was something behind Paul's smile, but was uncertain as to what kind of revelation was about to be made.

"Good morning, Paul," she replied rather hesitantly, "yes, I should hope so, she works for me. Good morning, Caroline, what's going on—what's the problem?" Her eyes switched from one to the other, waiting for the punch line.

"Don't worry, there's no problem," replied Paul. "It's just that Caroline doesn't believe you are an old dragon."

"Has this person been winding you up, Caroline?"

Caroline's face started to blush, "I'm not sure if Paul is, or whether you both are."

"I'll put your mind at rest. Yes, I am a Dragon. I'm Mrs Dragon, to be precise. Has that been of any help for you? And by the way, Paul, please, not so much of the old!"

"You're a scumbag, Paul!" exploded Caroline; her face had now turned red, bright red. "I'm sorry, Mrs Dragon, for causing you all that embarrassment."

Sue's Dragon smiled and started to chuckle and ended up laughing, "Look, Caroline. I'm not embarrassed one little bit; if that's all it takes to get some humour into this place, I'm all for it. Unfortunately, I must bring you back to reality, Paul. I'm sorry to bring you back to the doom and gloom, but have you seen Pratt this morning?"

"No, not yet. Do you know what mood he's in?" Paul queried, "Although, as he's never in a good mood, it must either be bad or worst."

"I saw him go in his office earlier, that's all. Caroline, are you alright for work today?"

"Yes, I've got another box of those data slips to enter and some bits and pieces I need to do."

"I'll see you both later," added Paul.

All three of them separated. Sue's Dragon stayed at her desk, Caroline went over to her desk and started work, whilst Paul walked towards Pratt's office and entered. Despite the potential for further problems, especially after yesterday's furore, the rest of the day proceeded without further incident.

That evening, Caroline visited Paul again at his flat, and it wasn't long before both of them were sitting on the sofa drinking.

"I can't work with that Pratt. He's just impossible to work with. This project might as well have been produced by a load of Chimpanzees, for all the meaningful data Pratt has let me have access to."

"What about all that data I entered the other day? Can't you get at that?" Caroline enquired.

"No. It just seems to have disappeared. The area where you entered it has some data in it, and it's similar to what you put in, but it's not the same. So, unless you're telling me a load of manure, there's something going on that's of the hidden agenda nature. Even that entry about Julian West has gone—that's if you put it in!"

"Are you calling me a liar?" retorted Caroline, instantly going on the defensive.

At this point, Paul snapped from the frustrations he has had building up all day. He leaps off the sofa and turns to lecture Caroline.

"For goodness' sake! Don't get on your high horse again! I've got enough problems with Pratt without you flying off the handle at the slightest excuse. You can either work with me or clear of. It's up to you!"

"Don't you raise your voice at me? I told you the truth." Shouted Caroline in reply.

They stared at each other, waiting for the other to give way. After a moment or two, they both burst into laughter.

"What work are you on about, anyway?" Caroline eventually asked, after they had calmed down:

"One: Find out where your data's gone?"

"Two: Why did it disappear?"

"Three: What on earth is it all about?"

"And save the world at the same time?" added Caroline.

"Yes. I thought I might do that after lunch, if we get time," laughed Paul.

"Very funny, ha ha, how do you suggest we go about it then, clever Dick?"

"The data you entered the other day could not have just been deleted. Otherwise, why did it get replaced with modified data? It must have been done for a reason. I think it's been moved to a high-security area within the computer. The individuals who have modified the data have given us researchers only the information they want us to have that's why the reports I've been producing have always given the expected results."

"Who's they?" asked Caroline.

"The government, I suppose. Someone with a vested interest. I don't know. All the reports I've produced, so far, support the government's policies."

"Didn't you say that Pratt changed one of your reports before you had your access limited? Do you think he's tied up in this?"

"Yes, he did, didn't he?" Said Paul thoughtfully. "That's interesting; in that case, it might be a group of civil servants, who want this government to stay in power, and not the government itself. Whoever it is, they must have some influence over the workings of the computer."

"Do you think Pratt could be involved?"

"Who knows, he's so nasty, you could argue it both ways. Let's forget about him for the moment and worry about the disappearance of this data. This is where I need your help."

"You mean you need little old me! I thought you just wanted me along for company—someone to shout at the appropriate moment."

"Come on. If you really thought that you'd have walked out ages ago."

"You better believe it," replied Caroline.

"Let's assume that the data has not been deleted; if it has, what's the point of producing those false data slips? Could you hack into the computer and find out where that data is?" Paul asked.

"No problem."

"And get some of the data out, not enough to be noticed though." "If I find any, I'll get some out. I'll start by having a search around on the computer tomorrow."

"No. No, hang on, that may not be a good idea."

"Why not?"

"Two reasons. During the day, Smithson is there. If he already thinks I'm a risk, which is what I suspect Pratt has already suggested to him, then he will be watching what activity I'm up to on the computer. And, if he's any good at his job, he'll also be watching those whose passwords he thinks I might have gotten hold of—yours, for example. The other thing that's worrying me is that car that nearly hit me. If I've become a possible embarrassment to this group, whether it's the government, the civil servants, or some other group, they may be trying to get rid of me. In which case, it could be dangerous."

"You'll just have to remember your 'Green Cross Code'." Interjected Caroline.

"That dates you! Anyway, if we try to avoid each other tomorrow and I'll keep my head down and out of Pratt's way, we won't draw any attention to ourselves."

"Then what? O' master."

Paul laughed and then continued with his plan.

"That building got enough loos and unused offices to hide an army. After finishing work as normal, we'll hide and wait until the night security staff comes on duty. It's an outside security firm, so they will only do what they have to. They come on about ten o'clock, if we give them an hour to settle down, it should quiet enough by about eleven o'clock. OK. So, we'll wait until then and meet on the top balcony overlooking the entrance area. Even if they notice any activity on the computer system, I'll be surprised if they do anything about it."

"And if they do?"

"We run like hell."

"That's what I like—a plan that takes in all eventualities."

"At least, it's flexible. Anyway, I'm going to bed; are you sleeping out here?"

Paul stood up and moved towards his bedroom.

Caroline called after him, "If what you're planning in there has been planned with the same precision as your plan for tomorrow, I shall be as safe as houses in my bedroom." She then fell about laughing.

Chapter 11

The next morning, Paul and Caroline arrived in the archiving area together.

Caroline went directly over to her desk.

"Good morning, Sue's Dragon," Paul called as he passed her desk and continued on to Pratt's office. Fortunately, Pratt hadn't yet arrived, so Paul was able to settle down at his desk without any cryptic remarks from Pratt.

Shortly after Paul had made himself covetable, Pratt came in through the door, glared at Paul, then sat down at his desk and started work.

At that point, the phone on Paul's desk rang.

"Hello, Paul Enfield speaking…Yes, I'll come down at once. Thank you."

"What was that all about?" Pratt asked.

"Nothing to do with you," Paul replied quietly as he walked towards the door.

As soon as Paul had left, Pratt picked up his phone and called Major Smithson.

"This is David Pratt speaking. Enfield has just received a phone call and was summoned to go somewhere I wondered if you knew what it was all about? Right thanks."

Meanwhile, Paul had reached the reception desk in the foyer.

The receptionist informed him that the chauffeur, sitting on a seat at the side, has come to collect Mr Enfield.

Paul walked over to the chauffeur.

"Hello, I'm Mr Enfield."

"Hello, Sir Gerard has asked me to pick you up and take you to his office."

"I'm ready to go now."

"Thank you."

With that, they both walked through the foyer and out the front door. The chauffeur opened the rear door of the Rolls-Royce parked outside and directed Paul to get in.

Major Smithson's had rushed down to the foyer and was just in time to see Paul and the chauffeur go through the front door and get into the Rolls-Royce. He went back to the reception desk and asked the receptionist what had happened.

"The chauffeur had come to collect Mr Paul Enfield."

"Who by?"

"He didn't tell me, but I overheard him mention Sir Gerard to Mr Enfield."

"Thank you," said Smithson, and he walked back to his office, deep in thought.

A few moments later, Smithson was sitting at his desk, wondering whether to phone Mr Pratt and tell him what he had just found out.

Eventually, he picked his phone up and dialled Pratt's number.

"Hello David, Smithson speaking…Yes, a chauffeur had been sent to pick Enfield up…well, the receptionist overheard him mention Sir Gerard. You mean you don't know who he is? He is a very senior civil servant involved in what the Department of Health does. More important is the question of why he has sent his personal car and chauffeur for Enfield. May I make a suggestion? Don't try to play games with Enfield, because you will lose." With that, Smithson hung up.

The chauffeur pulled up outside an office block in Whitehall, "I'll take you through to Sir Gerard's office."

"Thanks."

They went through the main door and stopped at the porter's lodge to obtain a pass that would allow Paul to enter the rest of the building. Having completed the formalities, they went up the stairs to the second floor, turned down a corridor just of the main staircase, and the chauffeur knocked on an ornately carved double door.

A voice responded by calling, "Come in."

The chauffeur opened the door and ushered Paul into a luxurious office.

"Paul, thank you for coming," said Sir Gerard, as he came round his desk, and shook Paul's hand.

"Do you want me to stay, sir?" the chauffeur asked.

"No, but please come back around two o'clock."

"Yes, sir," the chauffeur left, closing the door behind him.

"Paul, come and sit on the sofa with me. What do you want to drink?"

"What's the choice?" Paul enquired with a smile.

"Tea, coffee, beer, pink-gin or even champagne, whatever you fancy. I know, as it's a special occasion, we'll have champagne," he promptly went over to his desk, pressed a button on the intercom. "Please, can we have a bottle of champagne and two glasses, and could you also book two places in the restaurant for twelve-thirty…Thank you. Well,

Paul, it's been a few years since we last met. First, how's the flat?"

"Very satisfactory, thank you. I don't know how I would have managed to get a flat, especially a two-bedroom one, without your help."

"I'm pleased I was able to help; call it partial recompense for all the dangerous work you did on that Atlantic Island."

Suddenly, the office door opened, and the champagne arrived.

The person bringing it in placed it on a table next to the sofa.

"Thank you very much," Sir Gerard said.

"What do you want me to call you? Sir Gerard is so formal." Paul enquired.

"My friends, of which you are one, call me Sam."

Sam promptly opened the bottle of champagne, filled the two glasses, and handed Paul one.

"You're now thinking, 'what has he called me up here for?' If you are not, I want to know what you're on that's keeping you so calm and unflustered."

"Let me put it this way. You must have called me up here for a reason, and no doubt you will tell me sooner or later. So, until then, I'm going to enjoy this congenial and comfortable atmosphere you have provided," Paul responded with a contented smile on his face.

"I am very glad you are happy. From what I hear, your overseer is fuming and trying to goad you into reacting against him, so as to get you sacked."

"Yes, that is true. How did you find out about that? Are you spying on me?" Paul asked hesitantly.

"No, but I am keeping my spies focused on Pratt and Smithson and those around them, which is why you have unfortunately gotten mixed up in it. But don't worry about it provided you don't kill him, I can prevent you from being sacked," Sam clarified. "There, now you know why I wanted you up here."

"Am I at liberty to know why you are spying on them?"

"Yes, but first I must tell you your security clearance is way above what either of them have, but they don't know that, not for the moment anyway. However, what I tell you must not be mentioned to anyone but me, and only in this room."

"This is starting to sound interesting. Can I have another glass of champagne? As it will help me to be a better spy, like James Bond," I said in a facetious voice.

"Enough of the hilarity."

"Sorry. The drink, is probably going to my head."

"Pratt in particular has produced, or had produced, several reports, which indicate that every policy the government has brought out has been a resounding success. I noticed that one from last week, which, by the way, has your name on it, and even I knew it was wrong."

"I can let you have a copy of the original version of that report if you want to know what the real data shows," Paul offered.

"That would be a good idea. That computer terminal over there is connected to your system."

Paul went over to the terminal and logged in.

"That's interesting, on this terminal, I've got my original security level of access back again. Where do you want me to download the report too?"

Sam rummaged in one of his desk drawers, and extracted a memory stick.

"Put on there," Sam instructed.

A few seconds later, Paul's report was on the memory stick. As Sam replaced the memory stick in his desk, he announced, "I think it's time to go to the restaurant for lunch."

The restaurant was on the top floor, and after we had been seated and had ordered what we wanted to eat, I looked round and recognised several faces that I had seen on the telly.

"Sam, we seem to be mingling with several faces I recognise that I wouldn't normally expect to be on the same level with."

"When you have been involved in the kind of work you have, you deserve to be given a whole load of medals. So you are way above their respect level."

Lunch progressed at a leisurely pace and was accompanied by a rather pleasant bottle of red wine. When we had finished our lunch, we returned to Sir Gerald's office, arriving just before two o'clock.

"How can I get hold of you if I need to?" Paul asked Sam.

"Phone this number and ask for me; give the phone operator your name, and I'll have you picked up like today," Sam instructed, passing Paul a card with a phone number on it.

It was exactly two o'clock, when the chauffeur arrived to take Paul back to Victoria Street.

It was nearly three o'clock, when Paul walked into Pratt's office.

"Where have you been, Enfield?" Demanded Pratt.

"I cannot tell you, as it's nothing to do with you," Paul snapped back.

Chapter 12

Paul and Caroline arrived in the archiving area together.

"Good morning, Sue's Dragon," Paul called as they passed her desk, and Caroline went over to her desk, whilst Paul continued on to Pratt's office.

As soon as Paul had settled down at his desk, he picked up his phone, and dialled the number that Sir Gerald had given him; eventually, the operator replied, "Please, can I speak to Sir Gerald...Paul Enfield...Thank you," as he replaced the receiver. Pratt came in through the door.

"Who were you phoning?" Pratt demanded to know.

"Mind your own business," Paul snapped back.

Pratt went and sat at his desk without further comment.

About an hour and a half later, Paul's phone rang. "Paul Enfield speaking...thank you; I'll be down directly." Paul got up and started to leave.

"Where do you think you are going?" Pratt demanded.

"Nothing to do with you, and I haven't got time to discuss it with you," with that Paul left the office.

As he passed Caroline, Paul whispered to her, "I've got to go out, but I shall be back this afternoon. It's nothing to do with our project. But it will mean that we will need to postpone it until tomorrow evening at the earliest. I'll explain when we get home; it's hush-hush."

He walked down to the reception area and spoke to the receptionist, who directed him towards the chauffeur waiting at the side.

"Hello, Mr Enfield," acknowledged the chauffeur. And they both walked to the door, and Paul got into the back of the Rolls-Royce.

They drove round to the office block at Whitehall, where the chauffeur took him through to the porter's lodge for Paul to collect his pass, then up to Sir Gerard's office.

"Good morning, Paul, come and sit down," invited Sir Gerard.

"Good morning, Sam, I'm sorry to interrupt your morning," apologised Paul.

"Don't apologise, you're only doing what I've asked you to do," Sam replied. "I have also ordered a bottle of champagne, as you have developed a taste for the good life."

"Only since I've been seeing you," Paul responded with a smile.

"Anyway, I have been informed that there was a bit of an upset in your area yesterday."

"Yes, nothing serious though, and I wasn't involved. A few days ago, Pratt had convinced Major Smithson, in security, that I and Miss Caroline Aston are, in his words, up to something. Consequently, when even a hint of Caroline or myself having even coughed in the wrong place, Smithson and his trained apes are round like a rocket. All it was, Mrs Dragon logged into two computers at the same time, because Pratt distracted her. And as Pratt saw Caroline leaving the area to go to the toilet at the same time he insinuated she was to blame; however, Caroline didn't cower and confess, but made Smithson look rather foolish. Just another episode in Pratt's attempt to get the better of me and now Caroline."

"Do these little spats involving Pratt and you happen often?" Sam queried.

"About once or twice a day, but because Pratt cannot control his temper, he usually comes of worst," explained Paul.

"I see, interesting. Have a glass or two of champagne to calm you down, and lunch is at twelve thirty. Now what have you come to tell me?" asked Sam.

"Caroline and I were going to do some investigating tonight to find out where some of the data that was entered yesterday has disappeared to. But I suddenly wondered about you. How armour plated are you?"

"What do you mean?" Sam asked.

"Well, we postponed our investigation tonight because I wouldn't have had enough time to talk to you. Consequently, we have postponed it until tomorrow evening or sometime the next week or so. However, depending on what we find or don't find, there is a probability that if it is discovered that we have copied some very controversial material from an extremely secure section of the computer, we may be accused of causing a serious data leak, which may possibly cause a political row and some heads may have to role. There is also a high risk that even the government will fall. I just wanted you to have a chance to be out of the country on a fact-finding tour of Outer Mongolia, or something else, that will give you an unbreakable alibi, so that you will not be accused of being involved."

"That is very kind of you, Paul, to think of me," Sam acknowledged.

"As a further aide to you establishing your blamelessness, I'm not going to tell you how we are going to do it or when, only that it will happen sometime after the start of work tomorrow morning. I will tell you though, watch the television, and then you well know when it's safe to come out of the woodwork, or wherever you chose to hide."

"Paul, does that mean there will be no doubt as to when you have achieved your plan?"

"No doubt at all! Although, when you think it's safe, after all the backstabbing resulting from the blame passing has died down, please come and collect us and we will tell you about our adventure," Paul instructed.

"I can't wait. Time for lunch now, I think, and then I will disappear," Sam insisted.

Lunch was as pleasant as before. Although the menu was completely different. At two o'clock, the chauffeur arrived and transported Paul back to Victoria Street.

"Where have you been?" Pratt demanded as Paul entered the office.

"You don't have enough security clearance to know!" Paul snapped back.

Pratt obviously was not expecting that reply, as it resulted in his dumfounded silence. Paul just sat down at his desk and restarted work on his project.

Chapter 13

Caroline arrived at the office at twenty minutes to nine and went straight to her desk. A few seconds later, Paul walked through the open-plan area towards Pratt's office. He waved hello to Sue's Dragon and smiled at Caroline, trying to act calmly. Hoping Pratt intended to arrive at his usual time, Paul had come in a bit earlier to ensure he did not meet him. He wanted to avoid, as best he could, the possibility of any confrontation with Pratt, which could lead to a termination of the activities planned for this evening.

Much to Paul's relief, Pratt's office is empty, he goes in and emerges a few moments later with an arm full of papers and makes for his temporary desk in the open-plan area. As he switches his temporary computer terminal on, he sees Pratt coming around the corner in the corridor towards his office from the opposite direction. Seeing Paul setting himself up, Sue's Dragon gets up from her desk and comes over to see him.

"Good morning, Paul. I'm not going to be using my computer this morning, as I've got to see Miss Arkwright in personnel; would you like me to log in on your terminal so that you can have better access?"

"If you're sure you'll not forget and log in again later, I don't want to get you into trouble, and I'm certainly not in the mood to face Smithson today."

"As if I would. Move over while I log in. There you are."

"Thanks very much."

She walks away and leaves the area. Shortly after Paul gets up and also leaves the area, away from Pratt's office. A few seconds later, on the way back to her desk, Sue's Dragon passes Pratt's office. As she's passing Pratt bursts out of his office.

"Have you seen my research assistant? He seems to be spending a lot of time in your area lately." Pratt asked sourly.

Noticing Paul is not at his desk, she replies, "Not since he arrived first thing."

"I bet he's skiving."

"He's probably gone to check something."

"Probably chasing a bit of skirt. I noticed he was chatting with your new tart Aston again the other day. You want to watch him."

"I'm not listening to your nastiness find him yourself."

She strides round to her desk and, without thinking, starts to log in. As she hits the Enter key, she realises what she's done.

She immediately rushes over towards Paul's desk, calling to Caroline on the way.

"Caroline, quick, help me get Paul's stuff off this desk before Smithson and his idiots get here."

Caroline joins Sue's Dragon at Paul's desk.

"What's happened? Is Paul in trouble?"

"He will be, if Smithson thinks he's been working here."

"Why?"

"As I wasn't using my computer this morning, I logged him on as me—it gives him better access—and that ignorant Pratt. He made me forget, and I logged in a second time on my own computer. Shove this stuff in your desk, then try and find him and warn him not to come back here for an hour or so."

The phone rings in Pratt's office, and he answers the phone.

"Yes!"

"Hallo, Major Smithson."

"Enfield, no, he's not here at the moment. Why?"

"Really, I've not seen him all morning. Hang on, I have a look in the archive office; he has been hanging around out there a lot lately."

Pratt puts the phone on the desk and goes outside. As he emerges from his office and scans the open-plan area. He sees Sue's Dragon standing over the computer terminal on Paul's auxiliary desk and, at the same time, notices Caroline disappearing out at the far end of the open-plan area.

Pratt shouts at Sue's Dragon across the office, "What are you up to?"

"Mind your own business! Crawl back in your own hole." Came back the reply.

The rest of the office applauds, and a resentful Pratt mumbles something and returns back into his office.

Picking the phone up, "You still there, Major? He's not out there, but I'm sure something's going on. I saw that new girl, Caroline Aston, disappearing out of the office."

Two security men burst into the office.

"Your men have just arrived," continued Pratt.

Pratt hung up and turned to address the security men.

"I'm certain that something was going on, but I don't know what."

Meanwhile, as Caroline searches along a corridor on the second floor, she sees Paul disappearing into a copier room. She follows him in.

"You must stay away from the office for the next hour or so."

"Why? If I stay away too long, Pratt will miss me."

"That's just the point. He's already missed you. It's Mrs Dragon's fault; Pratt had a go at her, and she logged in again. I have stuffed all your bits into my desk. She told me to come and find you and tell you not to come back for at least an hour."

"Right, you go back. Try and get my stuff away from your desk. Smithson may get into his head to search all the desks in the office."

"I think Mrs Dragon was going to pretend she did it by accident. What I don't understand is that, as I was leaving, Pratt came out and shouted at her. How did he know about it so quickly?"

"Only from Smithson, which means they are more than just friends. Go on, get back. Say you've been to the loo or something. I'll disappear for a bit longer."

Back in the general archive office, Major Smithson is standing next to Sue's Dragon, who is seated at her desk. The two security men are stationed at each end of the office.

"I tell you. I just forgot I had logged in over there."

"Tell me how it happened again." Pressurised Smithson.

In a vexed voice, Sue's Dragon started her account again. "I was working over there; I went to see Miss Arkwright in personnel. As I came back, Mr Pratt came out of his office and said something in his normal offensive way, which annoyed me. That made me forget I had logged in over there, so I logged in here. Was that story the same as the last time?"

"I'll let you know after I've checked it out."

Noticing Caroline has just returned back into the office. Major Smithson continues. "Miss Aston, may I ask where you've just been."

Caroline antagonistically retorted, "I can't stop you asking."

"That is correct, but I'm also entitled to an answer. So where have you been?"

"Having a dump! Do you want to know any other details?"

"No, I don't think so at this point. Thank you. Would you mind if I had a look at what's on your desk?"

"And if I do?"

"I shall still have a look, whether you like it or not."

Caroline and Smithson walk over to her desk, and he starts to go through the piles of paper on it. Desperate to prevent Smithson from looking through the drawers on her desk, where she has put Paul's papers, she tries another tactic.

Raising her voice for all to hear, Caroline said, "You're going to plant something that will get me the sack, aren't you?"

"Why would I do that, Miss Aston?"

"Because you're a friend of Mr Blackstone."

"What on earth has that got to do with you?"

"Because he's under investigation for sexually harassing me. Therefore, if I get the sack—he gets let off. Isn't that what you're up to?"

"That's more than my job's worth."

"I reckon you, or one of your trained apes, have already planted the evidence whilst I was out of the office, and this pantomime is just to make it look good. I want personnel and the union representatives up here to witness this dramatic finding of yours."

Smithson whispers in Caroline's ear. "Either you are very clever or very stupid, I'm not sure which, but I shall be watching you." Then continuing in a loader voice. "I don't think that will be necessary; I was only doing my job. Mrs Dragon, please try to remember which terminal you are logged into in the future."

Smithson and his two security men leave the area. Sue's Dragon went over to Caroline.

"Well done, Caroline; you were brilliant."

"I've never been so scared in all my life."

"I'm sure Mr Pratt and Major Smithson are involved in something. And I also think that you and Paul are as well."

"I don't know what you mean," replied Caroline, trying to put an angelic look on her face.

"Let me just point out that you won't be able to call my bluff as easily as you did Smithson's. I do want you to remember though; I'm on your side if you need any help."

An hour or so later, Pratt's phone rings again.

"Yes! Speaking. Hallo Major. No, I've got no idea what Enfield and Aston are up to. Whatever it is, it probably involves sex." Paul comes into the office, and Pratt hangs up.

"Where have you been?" snaps Pratt.

"In the library doing some background reading for this project. I don't believe the data on the computer is right. So, I'm checking on past reports to see what they say about it."

"I want you in this office where I can see you and what you're up to. Major Smithson has been looking for you."

Sarcastically, Paul asks, "Has he now, and what did he want me for? I'm sure he would have told you, because you're his closest friend."

"I've no doubt he'll tell you when he sees you." Paul moves towards the door.

"Sorry, I've not got time to see him today. I've made a reservation at the library."

Paul promptly leaves the office before Pratt can object. However, as the door closes, Pratt immediately picks up his telephone receiver and dials Major Smithson's number.

"Major Smithson? This is David Pratt. Paul Enfield was just here; he said he was going to the library."

It takes Paul about ten minutes to reach the DoH research library. He enters and goes to the librarian's desk. As he approaches, the librarian recognises him.

"Ah. Mr Enfield, those reports you requested are over on that reading table over there," the librarian indicated by pointing at it.

"Thanks. Has there been anyone asking for me?"

"Not as far as I'm aware, sorry."

Paul goes over to the indicated reading table and starts going through the old reports. Out of the corner of his eye, he notices that the security camera is panning round. It stopped, as its lens pointed directly at him.

"Nice one, Pratt. So, you are working with Smithson," mumbles Paul to himself.

Back in Pratt's office, his phone rings.

"Hello, Pratt speaking…Hello Smithson. So Enfield is working in the library. Will you be watching him all day? That should catch him out if he tries to do anything clever. Thank you, and please keep me informed."

Paul continued to read the various reports the library had retrieved for him until it was about four thirty; he then packed them up and took them back to the Liberian.

"Thank you, Mr Enfield, for bringing them back; many don't bother and leave them on the reading table, so I'm appreciating you doing so." The librarian commented.

"It was no problem whatsoever," Paul responded.

As Paul left the library, he glanced up at the security camera and noticed it was still pointing at the reading desk where he had been working. Paul thus assumed that Smithson was no longer watching him. Consequently, he walked as briskly as possible, without arousing attention from anyone else in the corridor, to the opposite end of the corridor. He then checked for the position of the security cameras in that area, spotting one pointing away from him. He dived down a set of back stairs and went into an empty office on the first floor. After waiting for an hour or so, he walked to the stairs he had originally come up when he first started work, then he went down them, and hid in the empty office opposite the security office, which was now in total darkness, indicating that Smithson had gone home.

"Waiting for time to pass certainly drags," Paul thought to himself. "I wonder how Caroline is getting on?"

Paul kept glancing at his watch after what seemed to be every half-hour, only to find only about fifteen minutes had passed.

Chapter 14

The clock over the reception desk in the DoH building's foyer showed eleven o'clock. Caroline had already arrived on the balcony as Paul arrived.

"How did you get on?" Paul asked in a low voice.

"Not bad; I've only sat in six loos. What about you? Did Smithson find you in the end?"

"Not in person, but I let him watch me in the library all afternoon—on the security camera. Then I hid in the deserted office, opposite the Security Department, until just now. Hopefully, he thinks he lost me in the homeward rush."

"If he still thinks you're in the building, what then?" Caroline asked.

"If he thought that he would still be here, but I saw him leave about Six Thirty. Happy?"

"No."

"Come on, if we go down past personnel and up the back stairs, we'll miss the security cameras."

They walked slowly to avoid making too much noise on the stone floor of the corridor. As they approached the door to the personnel office suit, Caroline noticed something was not right.

"There's a light on in Miss Arkwright's office."

"How do you know it's her office?"

"Because I've been in and out of it enough times. Look, the door to the secretary's office is ajar; let's see what's going on."

"Now who's complicating things?"

After checking the secretary's office was empty, both of them slipped in and crawled under one of the desks. The light in Jasmine Arkwright's office shone through the gap left between the door and its frame, where it was not quite closed. Lying on the floor, they tried to catch a glimpse of who was in the inner office, but the limited size of the gap prevented it. If it were not for the sighs and grunts emanating from within the office, they would have thought it was empty.

"Are those noises what I think they are?" Whispered Paul into Caroline's ear.

"It sounds like someone is really on the job." Caroline whispered back.

"That's what I thought. Hang on a moment, do you recognise those voices?"

Forgetting to whisper, Caroline blurted out, "Bloody hell! It's Miss Arkwright and Pratt. What a combination!" Suddenly, it seemed to go very quiet in the inner office. Both of them held their breath, expecting Jasmine and Pratt to rush out and discover them. Eventually they heard Jasmine's voice.

"David, what was that noise?"

"I didn't hear anything. Come on, my dearest, stop worrying; we've never been caught before. I've fixed it so we won't be disturbed." Came Pratt's response.

"I'm not surprised he didn't hear anything; with all that noise they were making." Said Caroline, remembering to whisper this time.

"Shush. I wonder if we can find anything that we could use to prove what they are up to."

"If we had a camera, we could take pictures."

"Yes, but we haven't. Think."

"What about a recording? There's a tape recorder up on the desk. We could record all this noise."

"Brilliant! Get it down."

Caroline reached up and lifted the tape recorder from the desk and placed it on the floor.

"If we set it going now, it'll record all this noise. Then, when they finish and come out here, hopefully, they'll speak to each other, and that will identify them. Then we can come back later and get the tape after we've finished with the computer."

They set the tape recorder up in a position that would not be noticed by anyone coming out of the inner office, set it going, and left. They continued their journey round to the general archive office. It's in darkness, apart from a few security lights. Caroline sits at Sue's Dragon's desk and starts working at her computer terminal. Paul walks back and forth, from one end of the area to the other, checking for the possible approach of one of the security guards.

"Have you got in yet?"

"Not yet. For goodness' sake, you're like a pregnant father, walking up and down there."

Suddenly, Paul rushes over to where Caroline is.

"Quick, get under the desk; someone's coming."

They both scramble behind one of the desks, out of view of anyone passing through the area. Footsteps can be heard approaching.

"Paul, the terminal, switch the terminal off. The light from the screen is shining on the wall. Can't you see it?"

The click from the switch, as Paul turned it off, sounded like a clap of thunder in the silent office. The footsteps pause.

"He's heard it," whispered Caroline.

They strain to hear what the owner of the footsteps is doing. There's a jingle of keys, and the door to Pratt's office opens and closes. Paul crawls along the floor under the desks and looks down the corridor towards his office. The light from inside the office is shining under the door. Paul crawls back to Caroline.

"Someone is in Pratt's office," he whispered.

"I'd work that much out," she replied sarcastically.

At that point, Pratt's office door opens and closes again. Another jingle of keys, and the footsteps start to come towards the general archive office. A silhouette passes between them and one of the security lights. The footsteps pass and disappear and down the corridor at the other end of the area.

"That was Pratt," Paul observed, "I suppose he and Miss Arkwright has finished, but why did he come up to his office?"

"Who knows? Come and look at what I've found. Switch that terminal back on."

"You've found that missing data?"

"Yes, and much more. There's a whole area that even Pratt's not allowed to access. He and Smithson have got the highest security access, by the way. Look at what this letter says."

"I knew something was wrong. We haven't got time to read all this now. Can you get it to print out on the laser printer over there?"

"Easily. Just make sure it's full of paper."

Paul crams as much paper as possible into the printer's paper tray and closes it.

"It's back online now. Print as much out as you can. I'm going back to get that tape from personnel. See you in a bit."

"Be careful."

Paul rushed back down to the personnel office. Extracted the tape from the recorder and replaced the recorder back on the desk. Suddenly, he hears footsteps approaching and hides under the desk. The door opens, and a security guard comes in. His portable radio hisses and crackles as he switches it on and speaks into it.

"Hallo Joe, the lights are off, and there's no one here now. I'll come back, and you can start your rounds again."

As soon as the security guard had left, Paul raced back up the stairs to Caroline. His arrival, as he rushes into the area, makes Caroline jump.

"You scared the living day lights out of me," she snaps at him.

"No time for that. Have you finished?"

"I've one more to do."

"Get a move on then. Pratt must have bribed the security staff to stop doing their rounds whilst there's a light on in the personnel office. I heard the guard radio his mate to start going on his rounds again. That means we have only a few moments to get out."

"There, that's the last. I'll just shut it all down, and we can then go, and hopefully no one will know we've been in."

Later that same night, having made a hurried but careful exit from the DoH building, Paul and Caroline were sitting on the sofa in Paul's flat reading the documents they had retrieved from the computer.

"This one's got the Junior Minister for Health's signature on it, remarked Caroline."

"This one's from the Head of the Civil Service. No wonder they didn't want them found. They detail a deliberate conspiracy to suppress and hide anything that might show the governments health policy isn't working."

"That's why they hid all those people dying from AIDS. Surely it would have been cheaper to build decent hospitals, then pay for all this cover-up."

"True, but it wouldn't keep them in power. They needed to be seen with a health policy, among other things, that's working. It's probably the one single thing that got them elected last time."

"Paul, we can't let this cover-up continue. We need to get this stuff into the open somehow. How can we make sure that everyone is aware of this charade? Though, I suppose if we try to do it ourselves, the authorities, the government, or whoever is behind all this will move in and we'll just be squashed. Perhaps like the car that nearly had you. How are we going to publish this stuff?"

"We're not. The papers, radio, and TV will. First though, I'm going to see my friend at university."

"Why?" asked Caroline.

"Because it's possible to trace which laser printer was used to print these documents out. If they do that, it wouldn't be long before they traced it all the way back to us. I'll get him to scan them back into a computer and then reprint them on another printer. They can't check every printer in the country, only the ones they have access to in their various departments. We can then burn these original documents and post the new copies to the media."

Chapter 15

Because of their late night, or more accurately, their early morning retirement to the arms of Morpheus, they arrived a bit later than their normal start time. Sue's Dragon gave them a knowing smile as they walked by.

However, Paul anticipated something different would come from Pratt.

"Where have you been? Do you know what time it is?" Pratt demanded.

However, Paul was prepared for whatever nastiness Pratt would throw at him, "Wouldn't you like to know? But I have no intention of telling you. So what are you going to do about it?" Paul quietly interrogated Pratt, who's face started to exhibit its normal display of having been being thwarted.

"For your information, I shall be in the library. So you can tell your partner in spying, Smithson, which of his cameras to watch," Paul added to increase Pratt's frustration.

Whilst Pratt was fighting his exasperation, Paul left the office and went to the library.

"I wonder if Smithson is going to watch me all day today," Paul thought to himself as he arrived at the library.

Meanwhile, Pratt had calmed down and decided to give Smithson a call.

"Can I speak to Major Smithson, please," Pratt asked the telephonist on the receiving end of the phone.

"Who is that speaking, please?" the telephonist asked.

"David Pratt."

"Good, I was just going to phone you. Please come down to the security office directly." With that, the telephonist hung up.

"That wasn't Smithson's normal secretary; I wonder what is going on?" Pratt pondered to himself as he left his office.

When Pratt arrived at the security office, he knocked on the door and went in.

"Can I help you?" The secretary asked.

"I'm David Pratt."

"Good, please, would you sit over there?" the secretary directed him to a chair.

"You're not Major Smithson's normal secretary; is he around?" Pratt enquired, with a note of insecurity in his voice.

"He is in a meeting at the moment."

About ten minutes later, a man came out from Smithson's office, "Are you David Pratt?" the man asked.

"Yes, what's going on? I haven't got time to sit around here all day," Pratt demanded.

"You will sit there as long as I tell you," replied the man. Much to Pratt's horrification.

The man went back into Smithson's office.

"Could you tell me who that man is, please?" Pratt requested from the secretary.

"He will tell you when he is ready."

Pratt's face took on an expression of anxiety, and time started to drag.

Suddenly, Smithson came out of his office, closed the door, and went straight out of the security office before Pratt could open his mouth.

Another five minutes passed, then the man opened the door of Smithson office and called Pratt into the office.

Pratt was directed to sit in a chair in the centre of the room, whilst the man joined two other men sitting opposite where Pratt was sitting.

"Mr Pratt, it has been brought to our attention that you have been accusing Paul Enfield and Caroline Aston of, in your words, 'of being up to something'. As a result, a considerable amount of resource has been used to identify what that something is, but to no avail. We would now like you to elucidate what that something is, right now." The man insisted.

Pratt's face was now white out of fear of the unknown, hesitantly he started to make an account that he hoped would sound believable.

"Ever since he has been working for me, he has displayed an arrogant attitude towards me and has kept disappearing from my office, so I concluded he was up to no good."

"Perhaps," said the man, "you concluded he is up to no good because he has not been cowered by your attitude of trying to bully him into submission," the man probed.

"Of course not," Pratt was now being investigated in a way he had never experienced before, "I suppose you got all this false information about me from Enfield."

"No, as a matter of fact, not one of us three has ever met Paul Enfield or spoken with him. It's not true then that you requested that Mr Smithson should reduce Mr Enfield's computer access to public domain only, which would have made his ability to do the tasks you gave him difficult, if not impossible. Based on the information we have gathered relating to our research, into why so many of your assistance's have left working for you within a few days, we have discovered that you have desperately tried to make Mr Enfield react with violence towards you in order to get him sacked."

Pratt remained silent.

"Your silence shows that you don't disagree with that accusation," the man insisted.

"If you didn't get that false information from Enfield, you must have gotten it from Mrs Dragon," Pratt insisted.

"And who is Mrs Dragon?" The man demanded.

"She is a friend of Enfield," Pratt insisted.

"What led you to that assumption?" the man persisted.

"She always helps him, whenever he asks," responded Pratt.

"You mean they have a good working relationship, which you have never experienced, is that not correct? The question is what we are going to do with you to protect Paul Enfield and Caroline Aston from your incessant bullying. Have you any suggestions, Pratt?"

"All I can suggest is that I promise to stop doing it," Pratt put forward.

"And what do you think, Pratt, is the biggest objection to that suggestion?"

"I can't imagine," His voice started to reveal he was starting to relax, thinking he is about to escape some serious punishment.

"Due to your inability to identify what could go wrong, we are not going to implement your solution."

The man went out to talk to the secretary in the outer office.

"Please ask Mr Paul Enfield to come down to this office I think he is in the research library."

About ten minutes later, Paul arrived in the outer security office. The man called Paul into Smithson's office.

As Paul entered the office, Pratt immediately demanded, "What are you doing here?"

"Pratt, keep your mouth shut now you know why your suggested solution could never have worked," the man insisted. "Right," said the man, "this is what is going to happen. Paul Enfield is going to be promoted to Senior Report Researcher, and Pratt is going to be demoted to Junior Researcher, unfortunately, as you have not passed a BSc or a BA exam, we cannot promote you higher than 'Junior'."

"You do not have the authority to do that!" Pratt shouted at the man.

"Is that what you think?" asked the man in a gentle voice.

Paul immediately recognised the technique, as he had used it himself, and let a smile spread across his face.

"What do you think the alternative is?" the man quietly asked.

"To keep my existing position, of course," Pratt sneered.

"Paul, please go and ask the secretary to call two security guards to come in here and escort Pratt to the personnel office. Were he will be instantly dismissed for bullying fellow workers!" The man instructed.

Pratt's face went white with fear.

"Pratt, now you know what your two options are, I'll give you ten seconds to choose."

To focus Pratt's mind on the decision, Paul started getting out of his chair.

"Off you go, Paul and do as I requested."

"Alright, alright, I'll except the junior position," Pratt squealed, with a look of horror on his face.

"Now you will go up to what was your office, and you have fifteen minutes to clear your desk, and then you will leave the building. On next Monday, you will report to the reception desk in the foyer at nine o'clock. Please note failure to be there on time will mean automatic dismissal. Do you understand Pratt?" Pratt didn't answer.

"Do you understand Pratt?" The man shouted at Pratt.

"Yes," Pratt wailed, like a school child.

"Of you go then," the man asserted.

Chapter 16

The following Monday, Paul and Caroline arrived at the Victoria Street entrance to the DoH building at about a quarter to nine. They walked through the foyer towards the corridor entrance, at the left-hand side of the reception desk. They tried to look inconspicuously for Pratt but failed to see him.

"He may have come early or hasn't arrived yet," Paul whispered to Caroline.

They said, "Good Morning!" to Sue's Dragon as they passed her desk.

"Just a moment, you two. What happened last week? I have been told that Pratt will be working for me as a junior out here. And Pratt's name has been removed from his office door and replaced with yours, Paul, which means you have an office all to yourself."

"It wasn't my fault; I was just informed that I had been promoted. However, I believe it was because of how he treated all my predecessors," Paul said enlighteningly.

"I see," said Sue's Dragon, and smiled at them, "you had better go then."

Caroline went over to her desk, and Paul went over to admire his name, newly emblazoned on his office door, and then went in. Paul spent the next hour or so rearranging the desks and other furniture to his liking and then settled down and wondered what his new job title required him to do.

"I know what I'll do," Paul thought to himself. "I'll redo all those reports I did for Pratt so that they reflect what the data really reveals."

He switched his computer on, and to his amassment, he discovered he had regained his original security level of access, which he had on his first day. That is before Pratt got Smithson to restrict his access level to the public level only.

In fact, he enjoyed his first day so much that it wasn't until Caroline knocked on his door at five o'clock that he realised it was home time.

"Please, sir, can I come into your office?" Caroline enquired, in a frivolous voice.

"What's the new password?" insisted Paul, "And remember to approach me on your knees."

"The new password is 'You'll be lucky'." With that, Caroline spun Paul's chair round and jumped onto his lap.

"Now," queried Paul, "what would my new boss have said if he had seen that episode, whoever he may be?" "I wouldn't care," replied Caroline.

"As a side issue, how was Pratt today?" Paul asked.

"I was told he wouldn't be coming to our area today," Sue's Dragon announced, who had just arrived, without being noticed.

"Hallo, where did you creep up from?"

"Didn't you know I've been promoted to chief spy, to watch you two?" Sue's Dragon announced.

"Seriously?" Paul asked.

"No, I'm only joking. I saw Caroline come over to see you, so I thought I would come and join you. I hope that's alright."

"Was any reason given for Pratt's no-show?" Paul enquired.

"No, and I didn't recognise the voice either."

"I wonder what game he is up to now; I simply don't trust him," Paul announced.

"Are you coming home or sleeping here?" enquired Caroline.

"No, I'm coming home. Hang on a moment, since when did 'my flat' become 'our flat'?" Paul contended.

"I'm going, before I get mixed up in this pending row," Sue's Dragon, declared as she turned and left.

Caroline smiled and hauled Paul out of the office.

Later that evening, Paul phoned his university friend.

"Hallo, its Paul Enfield here…I was just wondering where you were with those documents I sent you…Good, so you will be sending them to the various recipients' sometime tomorrow…That's fine; thank you for all your help. Bye." With that, Paul hung up.

"The various media outlets will be getting their bundles of information sometime during tomorrow afternoon," Paul enlightened Caroline.

"I wonder if Pratt will be in the office tomorrow." Caroline asked rhetorically.

"We'll find out in the morning," Paul replied.

Both of them arrived at work as usual. However, after Paul unlocked his office door and sat at his desk, the documents he had left on in a pile on his desk were now in a different order from how he had left them.

"I wonder who has been in here?" Paul thought to himself.

Paul then opened one of the drawers in his desk and took out a clean sheet of paper. He listed the titles of the documents that were on the top of the desk onto the piece of paper in the order they were now and folded it up and put it in his pocket.

"I think I'll go and see if Sue's Dragon has had a similar problem," Paul suggested to himself.

Paul opened the door to go over to Sue's Dragon, when he noticed Pratt was sitting at one of the desks in the open area.

Consequently, Paul turned left down the corridor away from the open area. Went downstairs and ensconced himself in the empty office that was opposite the security office. Hoping the phone in the office was still connected, he dialled Sue's Dragon's phone number.

"This is Paul; don't say anything but yes or no; are you alone? Good, I see Pratt is in this morning. Will he be occupied for some time. Good, can you come and speak to me in the empty office, which is opposite the security office. See you in a moment, O' go via the ladies' loo, in case Pratt or someone else follows you."

It was about ten minutes later, when Sue's Dragon arrived.

"Now what's all this clock-and-dagger stuff all about, Paul?"

"Thank you for coming, I was about to come over to your desk when I noticed Pratt. I think he is up to something. Last night, when we left, I locked the door of the office. However, when I arrived this morning, the pile of documents on my desk was stacked in a different order than the one I left them in. Have you noticed anything funny like that happen to you?"

"Several days ago, some things got moved on my desk," Sue's Dragon divulged, with a huge smile on her face. "But nothing like you have described."

"Changing the subject, did Pratt tell you why he didn't come in yesterday?"

"No, Miss Arkwright brought him round, as if yesterday hadn't existed it was very strange. No snide remarks, no nothing he was even polite," Sue's Dragon remarked.

"Thanks for coming down to chat with me. I'm now going into the security office for a chat with Smithson about my office break-in."

Sue's Dragon left, and I went over and knocked on the security office door and went in.

"Can I help you?" Smithson's secretary asked.

"Is it possible to speak with Major Smithson, please?"

"I'll just go and see. May I have your name?"

"Paul Enfield."

With that, she disappeared into Smithson's office.

"He will see you now, Mr Enfield," the secretary said, and held the door open for me to enter.

"Come in and sit down, Mr Enfield."

"Thank you for seeing me so promptly," Paul said in a nice, polite voice. "Yesterday I was examining some files; when I went home last evening, I left them stacked in a particular order, ready to continue working on them this morning. I immediately discovered that the order the files were stacked in was different from that in which I left them. I locked the door when I left last night and had to unlock it this morning. Thus, I concluded that someone with a key had broken into my office during the night."

"Has anything gone missing or been changed?" Smithson queried, "As far as I can tell, nothing is missing, but I haven't had time to check for changes yet. I thought it was more important to inform you about the break-in," Paul elucidated.

"Quite so," Smithson concurred. "I think the best thing to do is for you to go and check for changes or anything else that's amiss and report back to me with what you find. Is that all right?"

"Yes, thank you for seeing me," Paul replied, and he left the security office.

Paul made his way back to his office and started to work his way through the files on his desk. At first, he didn't notice any changes, then on the third report, in which he knew Pratt had made some major changes, he found the changes had been stripped out and substituted with more appeasing changes. Although, the overall tenure was still in the government's favour, it wasn't as blatantly articulated as Paul remembered. He decided to go back over the first two reports again and look more closely, and as he suspected, they too had been modified, but by using subtler changes.

Chapter 17

Paul steadily worked his way through the documents on his desk, correcting the wording so that the conclusions in each document reflected those of the original ones before Pratt changed them.

It was about two-thirty pm when Paul had finished filing the documents, he had corrected, when his phone started ringing.

"Hallo…No, David Pratt's not at this extension number any longer. He is now in the general archiving area; I can get him if you want…I won't be a moment."

Paul went out and told Pratt he was wanted on the phone.

"Who is it?" Pratt snapped at Paul.

"I have no idea, It's probably one of your cronies," Paul replied in a quiet, calm voice. "Are you coming or not, or shall I tell them you don't want to know?"

"Alright, I'm coming." Both of them went back into Paul's office, and Pratt picked up the phone.

"Yes, David Pratt speaking. What! I'll be right down," Pratt stammered into the phone. Pratt's face drained as he replaced the phone.

"What's the matter? You've gone all white. Bad news?" asked Paul.

"I might as well tell you; you'll know soon enough anyway. There has been a bad security leak. Smithson's boss wants me to go down and meet him, because he thinks I might be able to assist in their enquiries."

Trying hard not to laugh, Paul said, "That means they think you did it. What have you done? I wonder what the visiting hours are at the Tower of London."

Pratt's worries over the phone call overrode all else, so he ignored the taunts. He left Paul's office looking guilty and very worried. On the other hand, as soon as the door closed, Paul fell about laughing.

A few moments later, having regained his composure, Paul left the office and walked round to Sue's Dragon.

"Hallo Paul," she said, as he approached. "What have you two been up to then? The whole building is full of rumours about a security leak. And Caroline has been sitting there as if butter wouldn't melt in her mouth."

"It's nothing you need to worry about, but be prepared for a full-scale security inquiry. Pratt has just been summoned to an interview with Smithson's boss, down in security, to help with their inquiries. I think the fertiliser is about to hit the fan," Paul elucidated.

Seeing Paul, Caroline came over and joined them, and the rest of the office congregated into various groups, discussing the different rumours they had heard, which were spreading like wildfire, and debating what the chances of them being correct were.

After a while, Miss Arkwright came into the area.

"I'd like to make an announcement," she commanded to the whole office.

She waited for the noise from the many conversations to slowly fade away.

"Can I have your attention? As you may or may not know, there has been a serious breach of security. It happened sometime during last week or so. Because of the sensitive nature of the information leaked, the Prime Minister will be making an announcement at one o'clock today, and then you'll all know what it's about. However, whatever the outcome of the various leads currently being investigated by security s, there will be an internal review of security relating to this office in particular. Therefore, I will be calling each one of you down for an interview sometime during the day. Thank you."

As Jasmine left, two security guards appeared in each of the corridors leading from the area.

"What are they here for?" asked Caroline. "To make sure nothing comes in or out of the area that might be relevant to their investigation. It was like this last time we had a supposed security leak. But it proved to be a leak at the treasury and nothing to do with us," replied Sue's Dragon.

Sue's Dragon's phone rang, and she answered it.

"Hallo, General Archiving Office. Yes, speaking. Yes. Yes, he's still here as well. OK. Bye." She replaced the phone.

Addressing Paul, she said, "Would you and Caroline go down to Miss Arkwright's office in personnel? Best of luck."

Having walked down to personnel, they entered the outer office together. The door to Miss Arkwright's internal office was open, with Jasmine sitting at her desk with a stern look on her face. To their surprise, Pratt is also there, sitting in the personnel secretary's area of the outer office. As all the secretaries seemed to have disappeared, there were only the four of them.

Addressing Pratt as he passed, "Haven't they locked you up in the tower yet?" Paul said provocatively.

"I'm in the clear; it's you two anarchists who are the problem," Pratt sneered back.

Jasmine's voice interrupted the vocal sniping, "Mr Enfield, would you and Miss Aston please come in here and sit down? Close the door on the way. Thank you."

They entered, closed the door, and sat down opposite Jasmine.

After they had sat down, Jasmine continued, "As you know, there has been a security leak. The leak consisted of a series of letters and documents, which have been sent to various papers, radio stations, and TV stations. The nature of the material they contained will cause considerable problems for the government. Hence, the pending Prime Minister's announcement."

"We've worked that much out for ourselves. What were the documents about?" interjected Paul.

"I don't know what was in them apparently, I've not got enough security clearance to know, which seems a bit ludicrous to me when every journalist in the country knows. However, I have been told that the only copies were in our secure document retrieval system, which is in a very secure area of the computer. After these documents were entered into the system, all, and I mean all, hard copies were destroyed. Hence, the only possible source of these leaked copies is from our computer."

"That lets me out, because Mr Pratt had my computer access limited to only the public domain. It was hard enough to do my job, let alone breaking into any high-security area," said Paul, smiling.

"Miss Arkwright, are you trying to put the blame on us?" Caroline asked.

"There is no proof at this stage as to who did it. I have been asked to interview you both because Mr Pratt told Major Smithson that he thought you two had been acting suspiciously over the last few weeks."

"If by suspiciously, he means we like and talked to each other during office hours, then I must confess yes, we did. However, I think you are hoping that we will break down and confess to something a bit more serious than that. Is that not so, Miss Arkwright?" Paul replied.

"If you're guilty of being part of this leak, yes. It would make things so much simpler. Major Smithson's boss has told me that heads must role."

"And Mr Pratt would really like it to be ours, because it would make things so much easier for him and for you, come to think of it. However, Mr Pratt was interviewed by three high-security personnel last week," I'm assuming you know about that, Miss Arkwright. "And I think you will find that they found enough evidence to lock Mr Pratt in the Tower of London."

But let us consider something for a moment, supposing no one in this building can be proven guilty. "What then?" Continued Paul.

"Security changes will be made to try and stop it happening again. But those who we are suspicious about may lose out on promotion or find themselves transferred to an out of the way place."

"I see, so you will be happy to condemn Caroline and myself on the grounds of false and unsubstantiated accusations made by Mr Pratt, in order to get himself off the hook."

A note of panic crept into Jasmine's voice, "I don't know what you two are up to, and I don't like the way this interview is going. It's obvious that you both know more about this than you have told me. I think it might be best if I call Major Smithson and ask him to sit in on this interview before we go any further."

"That will be just fine," Paul added. "However, if you call Smithson in, I want the three security men who were in Smithson's office yesterday in here as well."

Before she could reach for the phone, Paul smiled and spoke in a soothing tone, "Miss Arkwright, please don't rush into something you may regret very much. Look, it's nearly one o'clock have you got a radio we can listen to and hear this announcement from the Prime Minister?"

Jasmine got a small radio out of one of her desk drawers, and switched it on.

"I think Mr Pratt would like to hear this," added Paul.

He got up and called Pratt into Jasmine's office.

Pratt immediately snapped, "You've confessed then?"

"No, we haven't. Sit down and listen to what the Prime Minister is going to announce."

The Prime Minister's voice came over the radio.

"As a result of the revelations in the media this morning, concerning the government's health policies. I have accepted the resignation of several leading civil servants. However, because of the gravity of the accusations that have come to light, I shall also be having an audience with his majesty the king this afternoon and formally tendering the resignation of this government. The date of the general election will be announced in due course. Thank you.”

Pratt turned and shouted at Paul and Caroline, “Now look what you have done. I hope you’ll be pleased with yourself as you rot in prison. Jasmine, call Smithson and get this pair out of here.”

Still using a quiet, calm voice, Paul said, “Before you do anything rash, I think you had better listen to this tape first. Get the recorder from the other room, please, Caroline.”

Caroline got up and collected the recorder from the secretary’s area and gave it to Paul. She then went and checked that the outer office door was closed, then returned and closed Jasmine’s office door. Paul set the recorder up on Jasmine’s desk and started the tape. They all listened in silence to an audio manifestation of nonverbal pornography. However, despite the lack of spoken words, there is no mistaking the participants of the performance.

For a few moments after the tape had finished, they sat in silence.

Pratt and Jasmine looked at each other in shock.

Paul eventually broke the silence; “I made this recording between eleven and twelve o’clock during one night last week. Mr Pratt, you bribed the security guards to stop doing their rounds whilst there were lights on in this office area.”

“Were you here for the whole duration of that tape?” Pratt asked. The previous loud indignation and self-righteousness had gone in its place was the sheepish voice of a schoolboy who had been caught behind the bike shed doing something he should be ashamed of.

"No. After we discovered you and what you were doing, we set up the recorder. Went and did what we had to do and then came back to get it, after you had gone."

"Why did you record us?" Jasmine hesitantly enquired.

Caroline replied, "Because of Mr Pratt. He was being so obnoxious to Paul and myself that we thought we might use it to get him off our backs."

"You've brought down the best government this country has ever had. You've probably destroyed Jasmine's and my career. What more do you want?" Pratt whined.

Paul's frustration boiled over. "That's all you can think of—yourself and your opinions. This government's health policy, with its hidden agenda, has literally destroyed thousands of people's lives. I've been part of it, so I know what I'm talking about. Talk to Smithson and ask him about me and a small island in the Atlantic."

He grabbed the phone and thrust it into Pratt's hand.

"But don't tell him anything about what's been said here; else I'll make sure this tape will be heard on all the radios and televisions, as well as the content of the leaked documents." Pratt dialled Smithson's number.

"Major Smithson, please. Major, this is David Pratt. Can you tell what the connection is, if there is one, between Mr Enfield and a small island in the Atlantic? No. It's just that I need to know in order to try and find out who's behind this leak. So, you will confirm there is a connection, but not why? Yes, I know it's confidential. Are you telling me that, after all I have done for you, you're not going to tell me?"

Pratt went silent for a few minutes. "I see. What was happening on that island?" Again, Pratt went silent. "And Mr Enfield's role in this?" Another pause.

"I didn't know that sort of thing was going on. So that's why you wanted me to keep people out of the real data area in the computer and modify the data." Pratt hung up.

Chapter 18

"What did he say, David?" asked Jasmine.

"It seems I owe you an apology, Paul. I always thought you had taken those five years off as an extended holiday at the taxpayer's expense. Instead, you worked twenty-four hours a day for five years with dying AIDS victims, in some hell hole in the Atlantic, without pay."

"I knew about you working with AIDS patients, but Smithson led me to believe it was at a hospital," added Jasmine.

"So you now know that I didn't have to break into the computer vault to get that data, because I knew all about it before I even started working here. Never mind all that now. What I want is a cover-up for this leak. Caroline did the hacking that got the documents out of the computer. But she used Mrs Dragon's computer terminal. I don't want her to take any of the blame whatsoever."

"I'll see what I can do," said Jasmine.

"It might be difficult to do without Smithson on our side," added Pratt.

"I'll leave it to you two to sort out. But please remember, I've still got this tape," said Paul, waving the tape in Pratt's face.

After Paul and Caroline had left Jasmine's office, Pratt and Jasmine sat and pondered their next move.

"David, what are we going to do?" pleaded Jasmine.

"I think I know how I can get Smithson on our side, or at least to turn a blind eye. You check over things at this end and make them nice and tidy. I'm going to see Smithson."

Pratt went through to Smithson's office, knocked on the door, and entered.

"I wonder if I might have a word with you in private."

"Yes, of course, David. Come in and shut the door. Did you have any success with your enquiries?" Pratt ignored the last question.

"It's a very private matter, so I think this had better be off the record. Would you mind switching your tape recorder off?"

"How do you know about that?"

"It doesn't matter how I know. Just switch it off!"

Smithson went over to a small cupboard, opened the door, reached in, and switched the tape recorder off. He then closed the door.

"Leave the door open, so I can see it. Those things have a nasty habit of switching themselves on with the door closed."

"David, are you involved with this leak?" asked Smithson.

"No. But if you and your Bloodhounds continue digging, you will find that I'm involved in something."

"What's this something?"

"It doesn't matter what that something is; in fact, it's totally irrelevant. What you will find though is that the security of this building has been very lax over the last year or so, and that will concern you."

"And why will that concern me?"

There is a soft click from the cupboard as the tape recorder switches itself back on.

"I told you those things have a habit of turning themselves on. Shall I continue?"

"Hang on."

Smithson went back over to the cupboard and removed the tape recorder's power plug from the socket on the wall.

"Now that's much safer," said Pratt. "Let me put it this way. If you chose to investigate the security arrangements of this building, you will find that the security guards haven't been starting their rounds until all the lights in the personnel area have been switched off."

"Their orders are to patrol the whole building every thirty minutes."

"Yes, that was the original setup. Until you changed them, that is."

"I never did any such thing!" exclaimed Smithson.

"I think you will find you did. I have a copy of it, and it's got your signature on it."

"This is blackmail! I thought you were on our side."

"I was, until I found out the truth about this health policy we've been protecting. Don't think of it as blackmail, just an extended consequence of that corrupt policy. On the other hand, you could start looking for another position—times are hard—and a head of security, whose department has had such a large security breakdown as this on his record, may find getting an interview difficult. Need I say more?"

With a tone of relinquishment, Smithson relented, "OK. I'll call the Bloodhounds off and try and invent a convincing report for my boss. What else do you want me to do?"

"Open up the security level on both the computers in my old office, which is Paul Enfield's office now, so that we can access that leaked data legitimately. O' by the way, don't start that report yet I might have something for you to put in it."

"Anything else?" asked Smithson with a sigh.

"Yes. Rewind the tape in on that machine to the point where I came in, and we'll have a nice discussion about the coming Social Club outing."

Ten minutes later, Pratt walked up to the general archive office, where he found Paul sitting in his office. Pratt went over to Paul and knocked on his office door and went in.

"Paul, I have managed to persuade Smithson to open up the security level on the two computers in here, enabling you to access the secure area legitimately. I would like you, Paul, and Caroline to spend the rest of today and as much of the night as it takes to produce a report that includes all the stuff that was leaked. I've persuaded Smithson to call his Bloodhounds off, so you won't be interrupted. I'll go and see Mrs Dragon to make sure she is happy with Caroline working in here with you, and I'll be at my desk over there until you have finished. When you've completed it, backdate the report by three days."

Paul looked at him puzzled, "Why is Caroline going to work in here?"

"Because she's the computer expert, so you said, and I'm sure you would rather work with her than with me, considering how I have treated you in the past. Also, we don't want any more security leaks about what's going on, do we?"

Just after eleven that night, Pratt arrived at Smithson's office, knocked on the door, and entered.

"I think I found the source of the leak," announced Pratt.

"Are you sure? Our investigation hasn't produced any clues so far."

"Paul, who was my research assistant produced a report the other day, which included those items that have been leaked. He gave it to me just as I was leaving, but unfortunately, I didn't realise the security implications of its content and left it on my desk. I suspect that a cleaner or some other such person saw the report and pinched it. It's my fault for not locking it away." "Is that so?" Smithson asked sceptically.

Pratt signed to Smithson to switch the tape recorder off.

"That's the official line. Paul and Caroline have produced a report, which covers all the leaked data. It now looks as if we were about to blow the whistle on this policy ourselves."

"I sincerely hope so. I'm too old to start looking for another job."

"Put that recorder back on, so that I can leave and let you finish your report."

Two days later, at Paul's flat, Paul and Caroline are watching the news on his television.

The newsreader announces, "It has just been announced by a senior civil servant that the leaked document, which caused the current government to resign, was part of an internal report."

"Mr Paul Enfield, the new Director of Archive Research, said the original report had been produced by the department because of its suspicion that there was a long-term cover-up being instigated by certain government ministers. How the document was leaked is still a mystery."

"It has been announced by the Department of Health that all the offshore AIDS treatment colonies are to be closed with immediate effect. Closed wards in existing hospitals will be reopened to accommodate the patients. A spokesperson for the Department of Health also stated that a committee had been set up to look at the possibility of reopening some of the recently closed hospitals as dedicated AIDS treatment clinics."

"I'm going to bed what are you doing?" Paul announced as he stood up.

"I'll have to report you for sexual harassment. I do that to all my male bosses. It keeps them in their place."

A week or so later, Paul and Caroline were at Stansted Airport, watching as a plane landed and taxed over to where a line of ambulances were standing. Patients, who could, were walking; the others were helped or carried on stretchers to the waiting vehicles.

A doctor and several orderlies are supervising the transfer of patients. Paul walked up behind the doctor.

"I told you; I would get you a real hospital one day."

The Doctor spun round, "I know that voice—Paul!"

"Mike. How are you?"

"Paul, don't tell me you had something to do with this sudden change in policy."

"You'll never know. Anyway, when you have got things settled, contact me at this address," Paul gave Mike a card with his contact number and address on it, and we can organise a real get together, "I have so much to tell you."

The now empty plane taxied away from the reception area, another took its place, and the next group of patients started to disembark. At the far end of the runway, another plane started its final approach. Behind it, a stream of planes spaced out in a holding pattern circled the airfield, waiting for clearance from air traffic control to start their final approach. More ambulances joined the queue of waiting vehicles as the ones with patients in them left for their designated hospital.

Chapter 19

The next day Paul and Caroline made their way into the general archiving area.

"Good morning," Paul and Caroline declared as they passed Sue's Dragon's desk.

"Just the two I want to speak to," Sue's Dragon responded. "there have been all sorts of speculations flying around here over the last few days, relating to security and individuals being sacked. What do you know?"

"Well, nobody from this department is going to be sacked, not even David Pratt, and certainly not you. Therefore, there is nothing for you to get worried about. Although Caroline and I expect there will be some changes to security. So, you won't be able to pinch any more paperclips," Paul clarified, with a big grin on his face.

"What about you two? Are you going to stay in this department?" Sue's Dragon queried.

"Unfortunately, our future has not yet been decided. Or if it has, we haven't been informed. We have got a meeting sometime today about that. Hence, we are awaiting a summons," Paul said. I'll probably end up as chief sweeper-up.

"Could even be head tea maker," Caroline chimed in.

At that instant, Sue's Dragon's phone rang, "Hello, Mrs Dragon speaking…Yes, they are here. Do you want to speak with them…Certainly, thank you."

"You and Caroline are wanted in the foyer; I hope it goes well."

Paul and Caroline went down to the foyer, where the receptionist unexpectedly smiled at them and then pointed the chauffeur out to them, who escorted them out to the Rolls-Royce. "Mr Enfield, I'm not sure if you are famous or infamous; whichever it is, you have created quite a commotion around Whitehall," confided the chauffeur.

After a few moments, they arrived at Sir Gerard's office block at Whitehall. The chauffeur took them up to the porter's lodge to collect their passes and then on to Sir Gerard's office.

"Good Morning, Paul and Caroline, I'm pleased you both have come."

"Caroline, this is Sir Gerard, he basically runs the DoH," Paul introduced them. "Do I call you sir?" Caroline queried.

"No, you call me Sam. As Paul has probably told you, we only drink champagne up here, so would you like a glass, Caroline? I know Paul would."

"I have never had champagne before; will I like it?" Caroline asked.

"I do," Paul reassured her. "Try some; it's free," Paul encouraged.

Caroline took the glass and took a swig, "It's rather nice. A bit like fizzy wine but nicer." "So you like it then?" Sam asked Caroline.

"Yes, thank you."

Sam refilled Carline's glass.

"Come and sit over here on the sofa with Paul; I'll sit in this armchair."

Sam made himself comfortable in the armchair, whilst Paul and Caroline settled in the sofa.

"To start with, I would like to thank you, Paul, for warning me of what was about to happen when you were here last time. I had no idea you could cause so much mayhem. I'm glad I had time to get to Outer Mongolia. It was a lovely sight when I returned to see all those dying politicians and civil servants. I know that you, Paul, knew what was going on before you came to work at the DoH, but I had no idea of how or where to retrieve the evidence from."

"That is due to a skill I discovered Caroline possessed. We spent several hours looking around a very secure area in the computer. When we found how damaging to the government, it would be if a series of the documents were released to the general public, we decided to do just that and concocted a method of how to get them out to the general media," Paul explained.

"I see. Would it be possible to know what that gift is?" Sam Asked.

"Caroline, you can tell Sam if you want to. But you do not have to," Paul instructed.

Caroline pondered what the consequences could be if she told Sam.

"What you tell me, Caroline, will remain in strict confidence." Sam assured her.

"Right, when I left school, I trained as a professional computer hacker. And I became very good at it." Summarised Caroline.

"I must admit," Sam disclosed. I didn't expect that skill. How good are you?

"Consider, it took me about seven minutes to break into your top computer security vault. Is that good enough for you?" "Point taken, that is good," Sam pronounced.

"Before we go to lunch," Paul announced, "we would like to know how we stand as far as employment is concerned."

"Yes, I can understand that. Let us see, what are you offering us as a company:

- First: someone who can stand up to a bully and make him take demotion to a junior position and then be willing to take the blame for a non-existent data leak.
- Second: someone who can walk through computer security as if it was non-existent."

"How would I write the advertisement to find the replacements for you two?"

"Please answer my question in words of one syllable!" Paul responded with a voice that made Sam sit up and take notice.

"Paul and Caroline, please do not even think of leaving. You're going nowhere. The problem I have is, what am I going to call your new department?"

"Good. Let me help," Paul insisted. "The office where we are now working will do just fine. However, I will need the words 'Caroline Aston' added to the office door, in the same size lettering as my name. However, if you insist on vacating this office, we would like to move in here."

"Paul, when you demanded a reply to your question, the hairs on the back of my neck stood up, and I felt a shudder run down my back. No one has ever done that to me before. No wonder Pratt eventually succumbed and abandoned being a bully. Unfortunately, I'm not going to vacate this office. However, all the other requests will be carried out. Plus, the both of you will also be getting a pay raise," Sam explained.

"We both expect to get the same level of pay; if we don't and they aren't high enough, then Caroline will just go in and make them the same." Paul expounded.

"That is a consequence I had not considered when I confirmed your employment. Thus, I had better make sure your paygrade is high enough, as I have no way of preventing you both from getting the amount you will be happy with." Sam authenticated.

"I think it must be lunch time," announced Paul.

They went upstairs and were seated in the restaurant, and the waiter came and took their orders.

"I don't think I have eaten in a restaurant as posh as this before," Caroline observed.

"I bet all the people don't realise how powerful you have suddenly become," highlighted Sam.

"Not only that, but I have just realised that we could put salaries down as well as up; hence, you better not upset us," Paul added whilst laughing his head off Caroline and Sam joined in.

A group of men in pinstripe suits stared disapprovingly at us, tutted, and called the waiter over. Then the waiter came over to us.

"Excuse me, sirs and madam," the waiter said, with a smile on his face, "but that group of four men over there have complained about your laughing."

"May I ask who they are?" Caroline enquired.

"I will go and find out" the waiter said.

Shortly, the waiter returned.

"They said that they are members of parliament having a discussion and expected some decorum around them," the waiter informed them.

"I see," said Caroline, "I'll just go and have a word with them." Caroline walked over to the members of parliament.

"Excuse me, but I have just heard that you didn't like us laughing, but as far as I'm aware, you all still go to the toilet, which makes you no better than I am. So put up with it!"

Caroline walked back to our table and sat down.

"Now that is what I call a good laugh," Caroline announced.

The three of them and the waiter grinned, laughed, and then fell about laughing. A few moments later, the four members of parliament got up and left the restaurant, with the rest of the restaurant's clientele watching and laughing.

"Sir Gerard, of course I know who you are, but I'm afraid I don't know who your guests are," queried the waiter.

"This is Paul and Caroline; all you need to know is that they are currently the most powerful persons in this building, if not the world, and that includes me, you, and the four members of parliament who, just left," Sir Gerard explained.

"Are our starters ready?" Paul asked in quiet, gentle voice.

"Yes, sir," the waiter replied, and walked off, smiling.

Their starters duly arrived, accompanied by a complementary bottle of pink champagne.

"Compliments of the management," informed the waiter.

Having completed their lunch, they went back down to Sir Gerard's office, where the chauffeur was waiting.

"Sorry we're a bit late," apologised Sir Gerald.

"That's alright, sir; what happened in the restaurant is all over Whitehall." Informed the chauffeur.

"You two had better get back before you cause any more mayhem," laughed Sir Gerard.

"You know, Sam," said Paul, "that's not a bad name for our new department, 'The Mayhem Department'."

The chauffeur showed them to the Rolls-Royce, and they pulled away towards Victoria Street.

"Mr Enfield, I'm not sure what you are up to, but you two are certainly talk of the town, literally," commented the chauffeur.

"We'll take that as a compliment," replied Paul.

When they arrived at the DoH, they left the car, and the two of them walked up to the archiving section, hoping to slip unobtrusively into their office.

"Here you are," Sue's Dragon announced, and a crescendo of applause burst out, including David Pratt, from the whole department.

"I let you out of my sight for a few moments, and the whole of Whitehall is in an uproar. What have you two been up to?" Sue's Dragon demanded.

"We don't know what we have supposed to have done; please tell us," insisted Paul.

"Well, the story we have heard is that you told a group of high-up, egotistical members of parliament to mind their own business and vacate the restaurant they were in. To the applause of the rest of the customers," outlined Sue's Dragon.

"Is that what people are saying happened?" questioned Caroline.

"Yes, I'm afraid so."

"Let me tell you what really happened. There were three of us at our table and four members of parliament at another. We had just agreed on mine and Paul's employment conditions and were laughing at some of the unlikely consequences of one possible outcome. The four members of parliament called the waiter to them and complained about our laughing. Consequently, the waiter came over and conveyed the complaint to us with a bit of a smile on his face. I, little old placid me, went over to them and asked if they went to the toilet like me, which made them the same as me, in which case they would have to put up with our laughing. Then I went back to our table. Where the three of us and the waiter all fell about laughing. Some moments later, the four members of parliament left the restaurant to the applause and laughter of the rest of the clientele." I didn't know what all the fuss was about, Caroline concluded with a smile, "Although it seemed to be the best entertainment they had had in that restaurant for some time."

"Anyway," proclaimed Paul, "the thing I think you want to hear is the outcome of our meeting regarding our continued employment. I'm pleased to announce that we are going to continue full-time employment in this department; in fact, we are going to take over David Pratt's old office. It hasn't been decided what our new department is going to be called; I suggested 'The Mayhem Department', but we will have to wait and see."

Chapter 20

It was now Monday after Paul and Caroline had received confirmation of their new positions. As they hadn't heard anything to the contrary, they assumed they were still under the headship of Sir Gerald. Also, they didn't know what the name of their new department was, having assumed that Paul's proposition of The Mayhem Department had apparently been rejected.

"You know Paul; I'm beginning to find that this new job is becoming a bit on the boring side; what do you think?" Caroline proposed.

"Now, the excitement of the revelation has died down, everyday normality seems to lack the stimulation we've become used to. To be truthful, I'm not too happy with it either," Paul responded. "A similar thought that had come into my mind is that our special department, whatever it's called, is a device by which we will be parked out of everyone's way to prevent us causing problems."

Over the rest of the week, they finished going through the rest of Pratt's modified files and tided up other odds and ends left over from the 'leak'.

"If we don't get any positive indication about our future during Monday, we will reconsider options," determined Paul.

The weekend passed sluggishly and without focus.

Monday eventually arrived, and they arrived on the first floor.

"Good morning, Sue's Dragon."

"Morning you two, have you see your office door?"

"No, Paul and Caroline, responded in unison. Why?"

"Go and have a look."

Paul and Caroline walked over and looked at the office door.

"The Unresolved Department," Paul read out loud.

"What does that mean?" Caroline queried, with a note of suspicion in her voice.

"I don't know, but I know someone who does," Paul declared, unlocking the door.

As they went in, Paul's phone started ringing.

"Hello, Paul Enfield speaking…yes, certainly. Thank you." Caroline, the chauffeur has arrived to pick us up.

They went down to the foyer; the chauffeur installed them in the Rolls-Royce and transported them to Sir Gerard's office in Whitehall.

"Come in Paul and Caroline; I'm sorry it's a bit short notice," announced Sir Gerard. Come and sit down.

"Thank you, Sam," Paul acknowledged, as the two of them went over and sat on the sofa. Sir Gerard walked around and sat in the armchair opposite them.

"You are probably wondering what is going on and what your new role in the organisation will be." Sir Gerard proposed.

"That is true, and hope that we will gain some elucidation along those lines, this morning," Paul conveyed.

"There are many, what you would call 'old guards', throughout the organisation. Individuals who have been part of the DoH for a considerable length of time, possibly from its conception, and have become fixed in their view of how things should be run and dealt with. Obviously, some of them are an assist to the establishment. However, there are a significant number who want to make changes for their own personal benefit and gratification. What I would like you to do is find out those who are for the present order of things and those against. I have no idea of the number of people who are on each side," Sir Gerard explained. "Do you have any questions?"

"What sort of age group would they be in?"

"I don't know."

"Male of Female?"

"I don't know."

"Who were the three men who demoted David Pratt?"

"Hang on! That's a bit of a curved ball," Sir Gerard stuttered.

"May be? But I still would like an answer, please," demanded Paul in a voice that made Sir Gerard's face go white.

"You lead me on to believe that I could control your department, Paul, but it's obvious that there is no chance of me controlling it what so ever; in fact, I have let a monster out of the bag, which means all I can hope for, is that the beast finds I'm on the right side, whatever that side may be," Sir Gerard uttered, in a voice that was a lot less assured than before.

"That may be so. But I still would like an answer, please," Paul repeated.

"Alright, alright, there is a group of men who are responsible for the top level running of the DoH, of which I'm one the three who demoted David Pratt are another three. A further three were sacked as a result of your disclosures, about the AID's fiasco. I'm not at liberty to tell you who the others are. Some of them are working in various departments throughout the DoH."

"May I assume there is an ultimate head of this group?" Paul surmised.

"No, we work as independent isolated individuals or small groups, whatever is required at the time."

"Thank you, Sam, for your help. Is there lunch today?"

"Only if you stop questioning me, I find it so unnerving," Sam responded.

"Good because I'm starving," interjected Caroline.

We were shown to our table in the restaurant without any problems. However, when the waiter came over to the table to take our order, he recognised us from the last time we were in the restaurant.

"Aren't you the pair who caused a bit of hilarity last time you were here?" The waiter enquired.

"We are sorry for any inconvenience we may have caused," responded Caroline.

"Inconvenience? No chance, we thought it was wonderful the way you, with a dozen or so words, cut four stuffed shirts down to size. Now what would you like to order?"

The ordered food duly arrived, along with a bottle of pink champagne.

"I don't know how you do it," remarked Sam. "You either have people worshipping at your feet or trembling on their knees in terror. And I include myself in that."

The meal passed without further incident, and about three o'clock in the afternoon, they decided to call it a day and go directly back to Paul's flat.

Chapter 21

Whilst they were walking towards Victoria Street, Paul suddenly blurted out, "Last night, I was thinking."

"I suppose there's a first for everything," exclaimed Caroline.

Ignoring Caroline, Paul continued.

"I wonder if we could get Pratt on our side, because I think he has a considerable store of information inside his head, both trivial and significant. What do you think, Caroline?"

"I'll agree with you about what Pratt has accumulated inside his head, but whether or not he will allow us to gain access to it is another matter. How do you think you are going to go about it?" By this time, they were coming up to the archive area.

"Morning Sue's Dragon."

"I hope we aren't going to get another revelation later today," she responded with a big smile on her face.

"Not that we are aware of," they countered, grinning back at her.

"That's good, because I haven't quite gotten over the last one." A few moments later, they were sitting inside their office.

"I think I have a way to approach Pratt," commented, "Paul, in a cloak-and-dagger sort of way, using that empty office, opposite the security office."

"I suppose it could work," Caroline expressed condescendingly.

Ignoring Caroline's lack of enthusiasm, Paul led the way down to the disused office, opposite the security department's office, and set themselves up to hopefully receive David Pratt. Paul picked the phone receiver up and dialled the number for Sue's Dragon.

"Hello, Mrs Dragon, are you alone? Good. Would you please convey a message to David Pratt? Please tell him to go to the deserted office situated opposite the Security Department's office; just knock on the door and enter. Also, tell him not to divulge where he is going to anyone. Thank you." Paul instructed, and then hung up.

"How long will he take to get here?" queried Caroline.

"Five minutes or so," Paul replied, as he set three chairs into a circle.

Eventually, there was a knock on the door, and David Pratt hesitantly entered.

"Come in and sit down, David," Paul invited in a soft voice.

"Good morning, David," Caroline greeted him.

"It's nothing to be worried about; we felt you would be more relaxed if others didn't see you conversing with us. We wondered if you would be willing to help us in our next investigation." Paul clarified.

"That depends on what is?" David queried, in an uncertain voice.

"As you may have realised, from the new title on our office door, we have been formed into a department that investigates situations that have not been satisfactorily resolved, for example, the AID's scandal. Consequently, as I just mentioned, we have surmised that a number of individuals may object to being seen in deep conversation with us, out of fear of being dragged into situations they would rather not be involved with, which is why we arranged for you to come down here to talk with us," explained Paul, continuing in the soft voice.

"Will there be any records of who said what kept of these discussions?" David requested, with a more confident tone in his voice than before.

"Most certainly not, you won't even know who else we speak to, unless it becomes necessary."

"Alright, although I don't think I know of anything significant, I can tell you, conceded David."

"The information that has been given to us is that there is a group of individuals, not necessarily working together, who are intent on steering the policy direction of the DoH in directions, which would be of considerable financial benefit to themselves. Unfortunately, we don't know who they are, where they work, or what the possible policies could be. We are certain that you are not involved, but because you have been around for some time and remember things, we have surmised that you have a considerable amount of information inside your head, which could be useful to us. I'm sure you know what I mean—the odd unguarded conversation, overheard phrase, or similar things." Paul described.

"I see what you are after. However, there is nothing that is coming to mind directly; if something does pop into my mind, how can I pass it onto you?" David requested.

"We have used Mrs Dragon as a discrete messenger before, but she knows absolutely nothing about what we are involved in. Thus, I'm sure she wouldn't mind passing on a message in an unmarked envelope. However, I will check first though, so if you don't hear from one of us, assume everything is alright." Paul elucidated, "I think we are about done now; thank you, David, for your cooperation."

David left, Paul and Caroline set the furniture straight, Paul made his way back to their office via the long way round, and Caroline accidently bumped into Sue's Dragon in the lady's loo and gained permission to use her as a messenger.

"I think it may be sometime before we get any feedback from David Pratt. Whilst we wait, who do you think we could interview next?"

"I don't know really; what about Smithson? Let's see if he has any idea who those three men were who interviewed him and David Pratt?" Suggested Caroline.

"Yes, that is a good idea. Sir Gerard told us they were part of the group, so getting their names would be a step in the right direction. Come on then; there's no time like the present," Paul instructed.

The pair of them walked down to the security office, knocked on the door, and went in.

"I'm Paul Enfield and this Caroline Aston; could we speak with Major Smithson please?" Paul asked the secretary.

"I just go and find out," said the secretary, as she went over and knocked on Smithson's door and went in; a few seconds later she remerged, "he'll see you now." The secretary said, she was holding the door open for them to enter.

"Come and sit down. May I congratulate you on your promotion to your new positions?" Smithson announced.

"Thank you very much; it's a result of our new roles that I need to ask you some questions. I hope you won't mind."

"No, of course not." Smithson responded.

"Please cast your mind back to when you and David Pratt were interviewed by three men, here in your office. Did you happen to know or find out their names, or even just one of them, or their departments?" Paul requested.

"That is very secure information; do you have the requisite security clearance to be told that level of information?"

Paul handed him his security pass, and Caroline did the same.

Smithson examined them and gasped.

"That's the first time I have seen security passes with that level of clearance. I'm sorry to have doubted your validity."

"It isn't a problem. Now back to the question in hand, what can you remember?" Paul reiterated in his quiet voice.

"After the interviews, my boss told me the one that did all the talking was Mr Frederick Dawson. Unfortunately, I wasn't told his department, nor the names of the other two men. Has that been of some help?" Smithson divulged.

"Yes, that has been a great help; thank you, Major."

Paul and Caroline made their way back to their office.

"Can you see what you can find out about Mr Dawson, Caroline?" Paul requested.

Caroline started working on her computer. Paul went out and obtained a couple of coffees and took them back and joined Caroline.

"Is there anything I can do to help?" Paul enquired.

"Not that I can think of thanks. By the way, Mr Dawson is not in the normal personnel records, but I'm currently working on a set of records that are protected in an unusual and complex way, which indicates to me that there is something that is very sensitive in those records. That's it, I'm in, let's see what is in these records. Switch the printer on Paul, and I'll print them out," Caroline declared.

The printer slowly churned out hard copies of the secret files. Seventeen minutes later, Caroline started to close her computer down, which resulted in the printer finishing a little later.

"Paul, print some non-critical stuff from your computer to flush the data out of the system."

Whilst Paul organised his printing, Caroline collected her prints and started looking through the pages.

"Paul, this stuff is too sensitive to be left over night in the office."

"Right, I'll pack them up and take them home," reassured Paul.

Later that evening, the pair of them were working their way through the printouts.

"There are a wide variety of entries, some of which don't look dangerous, but the fact that they are in this group of entries indicates that they must be here for a special reason," observed Paul. "I've found two that are important: Mr Dawson and Sir Gerard."

"They don't seem to be allocated to any specific department, but Sir Gerald is the only one with a 'Sir' prefix, which in my mind places him as the one in charge of this group, and implies that he may not be as innocent as he would like us to think," surmised Caroline.

"We know a bit about Sir Gerard, so what does Mr Dawson's file say about his position in the DoH?" Paul asked Caroline.

"The heading marked 'Assigned Department' has the entry 'Unassigned' next to it." Caroline read out, "What does Sir Gerard's say?" Paul responded.

"The heading marked 'Assigned Department' just says 'Head of Department'. That is interesting, because it doesn't say what department he is head of." Caroline concluded.

"What do all the others say," Paul asked.

"Just a moment," Caroline said, and went quiet for several minutes as she hunted through all the other records. "They all say 'Unassigned'. I wonder if there is any other information in that file; I'll have another look in there tomorrow. Meanwhile, what are we going to do with these records?"

"What do you mean?" queried Paul.

"Well, Sir Gerard's not a fool, and I expect he will have realised that one of the first things we will do is to have a rummage through the computer. But, as he doesn't know what, if anything, we have found or whether or not we printed it out. If the material is as important as the computer security on the record files suggests, he will assume the worst-case scenario and presume we are now in possession of a significant amount of information. Consequently, he will have our office searched and probably your flat as well, which means we need to hide these records somewhere other than here or the office," Caroline evaluated.

"What's the time?"

"Ten-thirteen, why?"

"If we post these records to your address while we go to a pub. They will be in the postal system for at least a day before they are delivered to where you live, you do have a letterbox at your flat, don't you?"

"Yes."

"Have you got a big enough envelope?"

"Yes, hang on," Caroline said as she rummaged through some boxes in a cupboard.

They packed the records into the envelope and set of for a pub, popping the envelope into a suitable letterbox on the way. The rest of the evening passed pleasantly.

The next morning, they arrived in the office and tried to establish whether anyone had been in there searching during the night.

"As far as I can tell, no one has been in here," Paul concluded, "what do you think, Caroline?"

"I'll have a look to see if there is any other information hidden around the file I searched yesterday," Caroline decided. "That's strange that the file I searched for yesterday has disappeared." "What do you mean disappeared?" Paul exclaimed.

"It's just not where it was—gone!"

"Could it have been renamed?" suggested Paul.

"No, there's just no files here that could have been the file we are looking for. Assuming it's not been deleted; someone has moved it to a different part of the computer's memory. I'll need to start searching again, like I did yesterday, presuming nothing. It may take some time," surmised Caroline.

"Get started then, and I'll go and get some coffee," Paul declared, and left the office.

Chapter 22

"Caroline, it's near enough lunch time," Paul announced at about twelve o'clock, "what do you want to do for lunch?"

"I want to go for lunch somewhere, anywhere, away from this office," pleaded Caroline, "because I feel a bit constricted in here this morning for some reason."

"Come on then," Paul insisted.

Once out on Victoria Street, they started walking towards Victoria Railway Station.

"There should be somewhere we can eat and drink, in or near the station," Paul suggested.

The first establishment they fancied eating in was located on the station concourse. As it was relatively early in the lunch period, there were plenty of empty tables; consequently, they were able to find a place towards the back of the restaurant, overlooking most of the other patrons. They ordered their meals and drinks and settled down to engage in a bit of people watching whilst waiting for their food and drink to arrive. The tables were now starting to fill up.

"Look!" exclaimed Paul, in a discreet voice, sitting by himself over there in the far corner, it's Mr Dawson.

"I haven't met him," Caroline pointed out. "But I have met the person walking towards his table; it's Sir Gerard."

"Why are they meeting here? When they could eat for free, in the restaurant we ate at, near Sir Gerard' office," pondered Paul.

"Obviously they don't want to be seen together; I wonder why?"

Their food arrived at this point, interrupting their surveillance.

"I wish we could hear what they are saying," Caroline murmured.

"When Dawson leaves, do you think you could follow him and try and locate where he works in the DoH?" Paul whispered to Caroline.

"If I sneak out as soon as I have finished my meal, they won't notice me leaving; whilst they're deep in conversation, I'll then follow Dawson when he comes out, to wherever."

Once Caroline had finished her meal, she worked herself along the side wall and disappeared through the front door. Paul watched Sir Gerard and Mr Dawson make sure they didn't notice Caroline leave. Eventually, Sir Gerard left, followed shortly after by Mr Dawson. Paul waited about another five minutes, then he left and returned to his office.

Whilst Paul was waiting for Caroline to return, he had a sudden urge to reread the document he and Caroline had produced to cover up the AID's exposé. He went over to one of the filing cabinets, and after a brief rummage through the reports it contained, he found and extracted the relevant one. Settling back down at his desk, he started to flick through it to see if one section or another engaged his interest first.

Suddenly, there was a knock on the door.

"Can I come in?" Asked Sue's Dragon.

"Of course you can," responded Paul. "Come and sit down."

"Hasn't Caroline come back from lunch yet?" Queried Sue's Dragon.

"She said she might be late back; she had something to do. Now what can I do for you, or is this a social call?"

"Well, I have a sealed envelope for you, from Pratt."

"O' good, I'll not compromise you by opening it now, so we'll call this a social visit," Paul smiled at her. "How has he been out there?"

"He's a different man; he couldn't be nicer," Sue's Dragon revealed.

"I shall take my leave now and let you enjoy your letter." With that, Sue's Dragon got up and left Paul's office.

Paul couldn't suppress his curiosity any longer; hence, he tore open the envelope, extracted the enclosed letter, and started reading it:

Paul,

I have thought deeply about your request for information, and I must admit, my immediate response was to ignore it. However, in retrospect, I contemplated the way I had treated you when you first came to work for me, and despite all that, you believed I would be willing to help you. It astounded me that a relative youngster had that level of compassion and forgiveness. Consequently, this is all the information I think you will find useful.

A couple of years ago, I was in a meeting with some high-up officials who were discussing which direction DoH as a whole would go over the next five to ten years. There were four or five of these officials present, plus myself, Smithson, and three others who have since left the DoH; in hindsight, I'm not sure why we were there. One of the officials was named Johnson, another was Dawson, and another was Frances; the other two didn't mention their names and didn't take part in the discussion.

The final summary was that the DoH would endeavour to support the trends the government promised in their manifesto, e.g., reduction in AID's patients, although there were other diseases mentioned, which I can't remember.

I hope that this will be of some use.

Please feel free to ask me other questions I could help with.

Kind regards,

David Pratt.

Paul lent back in his chair to digest what he had just read.

"At least, it has given us two more names to work with, Mr Johnson and Mr Frances," Paul thought to himself. "We'll have to go over the documents we've printed out to try and glean some more information about them. talking about other people, I wonder where Caroline has got to."

Paul was just starting to become concerned about the length of time Caroline was taking to reappear, as it was coming up to three o' clock. He rested his eyes and drifted into a light dose. Suddenly, his phone sounded and reawakened, bringing him back into action. He grabbed the phone.

"Paul Enfield speaking. Caroline, are you alright? Where are you? Why are you at the flat? Right, I'll come home now. See you shortly, bye."

Paul folded David Pratt's letter up and put it in his pocket, tided the office up, then left to go to his flat and find out why Caroline had ended up there.

It took him about half an hour to get to his flat. He unlocked the door and went in, and he found Caroline lying on the sofa crying her eyes out.

"What's the matter? Why are you crying?"

"I lost Dawson; I've let you down. The first important task you gave me, and I failed," sobbed Caroline.

"Don't upset yourself," Paul consoled her. "There was always a chance he would give you the slip, whether it be by design or chance. Do you know where you lost him?"

"We passed the DoH entrance in Victoria Street, and I was about a hundred metres behind him when suddenly he turned right down a narrow turning, just past the entrance. I rushed up to the turning, but he had disappeared. The turning wasn't wide enough for cars and lorries to get down, but bikes and motorbikes could."

"Could you see if there were any entrances he could have vanished into?" Paul queried affectionately.

"There were several," Caroline confirmed, having now stopped crying.

"Caroline, are you up to walking back there now?"

After a gentle stroll, they arrived at the junction between the narrow turning and Victoria Street. There were five doorways through which Dawson could have disappeared.

"As the DoH building is on the right-hand side, therefor we can ignore the doorways on the left-hand side," observed Paul, "which leaves two doorways on the right-hand side to consider as possible candidates."

They walked to the first right-hand door; unfortunately, there was no signage on it; in fact, it looked like it hadn't been opened for some time.

"I don't think Dawson went through that one," Caroline remarked, "let's try the next one."

The second door had a sign with 'DoH Maintenance' on it. Paul tried turning the doorknob, which turned and allowed the door to open. He looked round the door and found it opened onto a dimly lit passage.

"This must be where Dawson went," Caroline whispered.

"It certainly looks that way," responded Paul. "This seems to indicate that he either works in this department or knew how to cut through to where his department is without causing undue disturbance. I think the thing to do is go back, and enter through the main entrance and try to establish how to get to this doorway from the inside. What do you think, Caroline?"

"That sounds like a good idea to me, but it makes me feel rather stupid for bursting into tears over something so trivial."

"Stress can inflict unexpected emotions on your awareness," Paul soothingly perceived.

They made their way back to their office.

"Caroline, when you started working here, you were given a bunch of documents, one of which contained a map of the building, do you have it here?" Paul enquired.

"Yes, they're somewhere in my desk; let me have a look," Caroline started rummaging through the papers on her desk, "here it is." "Spread it on the desk," Paul insisted.

They both peered at it.

"There's the Main Front Door," Paul pointed out, "If we follow the outside wall along until it comes to its end, then turn right, we should find a doorway or two. The first one will be the door that's not been opened for ages, and the second should be the one we are looking for. Look, there's the first door; it seems to just enter into a single room. However, there's the second door, and it seems to enter onto a corridor, which would make it the door we are looking for. Now where does that corridor lead to?"

"It's a bit vague as to where it leads," commented Caroline, "although, that area next to the corridor there is marked 'workshop'. The area on the other side isn't marked it's just a blank area. However, the unmarked area runs next to the corridor, which leads past the security office; perhaps there's a doorway in that corridor that connects to the unlabelled area."

"Fancy a stroll along a few corridors then?" suggested Paul.

Chapter 23

It was now coming up to six o'clock, and most of the staff had gone home for the day.

"We shouldn't bump into anyone, as they mostly will have gone home by now, but you never know," Paul asserted.

"Well, I hope you can invent a good reason for being somewhere you shouldn't be, if we do," Caroline taunted Paul in reply.

They made their way down to the security office and slowly walked along the corridor away from the main foyer. Eventually, they came to a door marked 'Authorised personnel only'. Caroline tried to open the door, but much to her surprise, it opened. They found themselves in a dimly lit corridor, with a series of doors leading to it. One door was labelled 'Workshop'; several other doors were blank. But unexpectedly, the last one was labelled 'Computer Room'.

"Now this is an interesting find," Caroline commented quietly. "I wonder if there is more than one computer in here; if there is, it could be where our missing files have migrated to. Let us go in and have a look."

With that, she tried the door, and again, to her surprise, it opened.

"The security is very slack round here, which indicates not many people come to this area," Paul intimated.

Noticing a desk with a terminal, keyboard, and mouse on it, Caroline walked over to the desk and moved the mouse to see what the reaction would be. The screen immediately lit up, and looked as if it was expecting some kind of input. Caroline sat in the seat next to the desk and started typing some commands on the keyboard.

"This isn't the general computer that everyone has access to," announced Caroline. "Give me a few moments and I'll see what I can discover."

Paul watched the terminal screen over Caroline's shoulder all he could see was a stream of computer program commands being entered. Suddenly, the screen filled up with files.

"That's more like it," announced Caroline, "they're the files that disappeared from the computer in our office. Obviously, they think this computer is more secure than ours. I'll see if I can work out how they transferred those files onto this computer."

More computer commands worked their way up the screen; eventually, a file directory with the name 'transfer directory', appeared on the display.

"That's how they did it; in our computer there is a directory named 'secure transfer directory', when I checked it yesterday, it was empty, which means they (whoever they are) transferred those files from our computer to this one, just after we printed them out," concluded Caroline.

"Whilst we are in there, is there anything in this computer that may be of use for us?" asked Paul.

"I'll have a look round."

As Caroline started work looking for files that could be of use in their quest, Paul started looking round the room, trying to establish who or what the room was normally used for, other than a computer room. In the far corner was a desk without a computer on it. Inquisitiveness got the better of Paul; consequently, he started searching the desk draws. Unexpectedly, he found a bundle of A4 envelopes, which he couldn't resist opening.

"Caroline, look what I've found."

Paul handed her the contents of the first envelope. A few moments later, Caroline looked at Paul.

"This looks like a smoking gun!" Caroline exclaimed.

"That's what I thought," Paul confirmed.

Paul took the contents of the letter from Caroline and replaced them in the envelope, then bundled it with the rest of the envelopes, so he could easily carry them. Caroline carefully shut down the computer she had been working on. Then both of them carefully made their way through the labyrinth of corridors back to their offices.

"I think we need to get these envelopes into your house with the other documents," Paul suggested.

"Let's get a taxi," declared Caroline. "I'll put these letters in my big bag, so they won't be seen when we leave."

The taxi took them to Paul's flat. Then they went into the flat and changed their attire, in case they were being followed, and then hired another taxi from a different company to take them to Caroline's bedsit.

They arrived at Caroline's bedsit, about nine o'clock in the evening. As they entered, they picked up the earlier package from behind the front door.

The rest of the evening was spent arranging the various documents into groups, either by name or subject matter, depending on what the main thrust of the document was. Paul then made lists of the names and their subjects, which resulted in an unexpectedly short list. Whilst Paul worked on his list, Caroline packed the heaps he had finished with into a corresponding order and hid them in an unobvious place. Next morning, they arrived back at their office in the archiving area at their usual time, as if everything were normal.

"I think I'll phone Sir Gerard," announced Paul, as he picked the phone up and dialled the appropriate number. "He's got some questions to answer don't you agree, Caroline?"

"Yes, I do agree, but my questions may be different from yours."

Whilst they waited for the chauffeur to arrive, Paul made a second list, but instead of names, he made it using numbers and then marked his first list with each number against the appropriate name. In due course, they arrived at Sir Gerard's office.

"Come in, Paul and Caroline," Sir Gerard's voice bid them to enter his domain, "sit down over here. Would you like some champagne?"

"Yes, please," Paul and Caroline answered in unison.

"This is a list of individuals we have put together and the diverse subject matter they have been associated with. What do you think, Sam?" Paul enquired, displaying his most disarming smile on his face.

"But there are no names on it, just numbers, so how can I tell who they are?" questioned Sam.

"You can't, until I tell you. We have done that because you are on that list, and we would like to know if you can recognise your own entry from the rest," Paul explained.

"I see," said Sam hesitantly, "you never make things easy."

"I find I get a better idea of the truth that way," Paul replied.

"Looking at the list of subjects you have provided, the only one that I would fully condone is number three."

"Are you completely happy with that selection and the consequences it may bring upon you, Sam?"

"Yes, I am," Sam responded, with a voice that sounded much more confident.

"I'm glad, because that is you," confirmed Paul with a big smile.

"That's a relief," Sam substantiated. "Please tell me where and how you retrieved that information. I assume you've got it in writing."

"Yes, we do have it in writing, but I'm not at liberty to tell you how we got it."

"There's no point in asking you, because I know you won't reveal how or where that information came from. Unfortunately, even I don't know where it was deposited. The point is, what am I going to do with this information? I'm going to have to choose between keeping the DoH funded by the National Health System or have it privatised. I noticed that some ministers have visited American health suppliers with a view to privatising our health system. We've got an election in a couple of weeks, so I think I'll wait until after that before I trigger a potential for another fiasco. Anyway, let's finish this champagne and go for lunch."

They were halfway through their lunch when Caroline asked:

"What would you have done? if we wanted to privatise the DoH and refused to help you keep it in the National Health System?"

"You two always ask difficult questions and seem to know when I'm lying," Sam responded, "in that case, I wouldn't know how to take you out of circulation. Thankfully, I won't have to find out."

"However, there is one question I would like an answer to now," Paul insisted, in a voice that made Sam's face suddenly drain of colour. "Yesterday you were seen visiting a Mr Dawson in a restaurant, situated in Victoria Station. It was observed as being quite an animated discussion, and we would like to know what it was about, please."

"Yes, I remember the situation," Sam admitted. "I was trying to change his mind regarding privatisation."

"Are you sure that is all it was about?" Paul's voice had become harder.

"Yes, I promise you it was only about that," Sam replied; however, his face was now completely white.

"I'll accept what you have told me, for the moment, but the colour of your face is telling me there is something else."

Having finished lunch without any further dramatic confrontations, they were back in Sam's office, waiting for the chauffeur to arrive to take them back to the DoH building.

"When you have decided what to do about the privatisation gang, I'll let you have all the information we have collected," Paul conceded.

"That's if we don't change our minds about privatisation," Caroline interjected with a smile on her face.

Sam looked at her with horror on his face. Unfortunately, the chauffeur arrived at that point, which prevented any further discussion on that theme.

"Goodbye, Sir Gerard," Paul said, gentle smiling however, he noted that Sir Gerard's face was still blanched.

Once back in their office, Caroline commented, "I wonder what Sir Gerard is trying to hide from us."

"I'm glad you picked that up as well." Paul acknowledged.

Chapter 24

"Hang on," Paul suddenly said, "Sir Gregory stressed it was a choice of two options, privatisation or national health, but suppose there is another option. He mentioned that some ministers had visited various companies in America. What if they had put together some kind of third option?"

"I'll have a look on the computer to see what I can find," Caroline uttered.

"That is a good idea, although don't forget about that second computer we found you may be able to connect through to it," Paul consented.

Silence descended as Caroline started scrutinising the computer contents for information relating to the ministers visits to America and their health practices.

"Whilst you play with the computers, I'll go and get some coffee," announced Paul.

As Paul left the office, David Pratt left his desk and followed him towards the coffee machine.

"Hallo Paul," announced David Pratt. When they had reached the coffee machine, the sound of David Pratt's voice made Paul jump, "David, you made me jump, how are things going?"

"Not too bad; I wanted to speak to you, and this is the first chance I have had."

"Do you want to meet in the empty office, opposite the security office?" asked Paul.

"Yes, I would feel more comfortable in there," acknowledged David.

"No problem, see you at the empty office at about three thirty."

"Paul arrived at the deserted office about twenty-past-three and waited for David Pratt to arrive."

Eventually, there was a knock on the door.

"Come in," Paul responded.

David Pratt came in and sat in the chair Paul indicated.

"Hallo David, how can I help?" Paul asked in a placid voice.

"As I suspect you are still looking for people who may be involved in inciting others to change their opinion of how the National Health System should be run?" David asked.

"Yes, I'm still very interested," Paul responded.

"As it happens, I have been party to a conversation on that very subject," continued David.

"Please tell me more, David," Paul encouraged.

"There was a group of five of us discussing what would be best for the users of the National Health Service and how it could be run to achieve that aim. Obviously, leaving things as they are was put as the default position we covered privatisation as a fairly positive alternative. However, we also discussed some other options, such as selling the National Health data contents to the Americans and using the money to fund the existing structure; another one was to sell the National Health in its entirety, and in return the Americans would run it in the same way as it is now. Interestingly, one suggestion was to wind the clock back and do away with National Health Trusts and re-establish the old structure with Matrons and the rest of the hierarchy. This means that there are six different options being talked about amongst the powers that be. I hope that this has been useful, Paul."

"David, I thank you very much for providing this extremely useful information."

"There is one thing I had better tell you, most of the DoH staff who were involved with the various options have now left the employment of the DoH, with the exception of Mr Dawson. Also, the original ministers involved in the discussions with the Americans have either left or have changed which department they work for. Consequently, I don't think any of the original minsters are still involved."

"That is very useful to know; thank you, David, for your help," Paul emphasised in a really positive way.

With that, David Pratt left the disused office. Paul made a summary of what had been discussed, tided up, and left to join Caroline back in their office.

"Hallo Caroline, have you missed me?"

"No, not really," she replied.

"Anyway, how's the computer searching progressing?" Paul enquired.

"Not much at all," said Caroline. "Apart from a few letters that confirmed some discussions had taken place and outlined what was agreed at those meetings."

"That's good, as I have got a list of six different options from David Pratt, and as far as he knows, only one person is still active in this field, Mr Dawson. How do these two lists compare?" Paul queried.

"Looking at your list, Paul, and relating the positive aspects with mine, we end up with the status quo and two alternatives: one is to sell the national health lock stock and barrel to the Americans; the second is to sell the on-going data generated by the national health and use the money resulting from that sale, which would probably be in the region of billions of pounds, to restructure the health system. That could be the third way Sir Gerard wants to achieve."

"I think you're right, Caroline. In the morning, we will see if we can go and confront Sir Gerard and see if he has thought of the consequences."

First thing in the following morning, Paul made the necessary phone call, and eventually they both arrived at Sir Gerard's office, "Come in and sit down," invited Sir Gerard, "I've ordered some champagne. However, I'm not sure if this is going to be a pleasant encounter or not."

"Well, how it turns out will depend on your reaction to our questions," responded Paul, keeping a neutral look on his face.

"I had a feeling that it might," Sam replied, trying to keep a gentile smile on his face.

"Caroline and I have made some discoveries since we last spoke to you, and they suggested that you may be hiding something from us. Well, we have in fact discovered that there were originally six options regarding the fate of the national health. If you remember you told us there were only two, but we have investigated and found that there are now only three viable options: the status quo; selling the National Health to the Americans in its entirety; but the third option was selling the National Health's mountain of data to the Americans in exchange for billions of dollars. What do you have to say about that, Sam?" Paul elucidated.

"I have no option but to agree with you, but as I said during your last visit, I support the idea of maintaining the status quo regarding the National Health."

"That's true, Sam, but you were hiding something, as betrayed by the colour of your face going white. So I ask you again, Sam, what were you hiding last time?" Paul insisted.

"I should have known better to try and mislead you and Caroline. Your third option is what I thought would be best for the long-term future of the National Health. However, since then, I have had a conversation with the legal people about what could happen if we adopted that option and sold the huge amount of data generated by the National Health to the Americans. Their opinion was that although we would have got billions of dollars for that sale, as time progressed, they would insist on more and more personal data being included, which would have meant that we would gradually lose control over how the National Health would need to be run. Consequently, I'm now in favour of keeping the first option, the status quo. And I assure you, Paul, I'm now not hiding anything."

"I know you're not hiding anything, by the look on your face," reassured Paul. "However, we need to address the insinuated problem, you inferred, concerning Mr Dawson. What exactly is the hindrance relating to Mr Dawson? Interestingly, we have so far been unable to discover where he actually works or what department he is attached to. I think we need some input from yourself at this point."

"Right, let us go and have lunch, and I'll try to expand your understanding of Mr Dawson," responded Sam.

They went upstairs and ordered their food.

"Come on then, Sam, where are we going to start with our discussion of Mr Dawson?" Caroline probed.

"Mr Dawson is one of the oldest executives at the DoH; I don't mean he is approaching retirement, just that he has been employed here the longest. There were some older than him, but they have either retired or moved somewhere else. Because of his age, he feels he has the right to dictate what happens regarding the direction the DoH policy should go. Unfortunately, he has friends who are deeply involved in politics, I don't mean as MPs, but behind the scenes to ensure that they, as individuals, would make considerable amounts of money. From time to time, these so-called friends have a tendency to try and mislead him as to what would be best for the long-term future of the DoH, which has needed to be overridden one way or another. That task sometimes falls to me. Unfortunately, this particular time, it's proving more difficult than expected to adjust his viewpoint, which is what the altercation at Victoria was really all about."

"I can appreciate your concern if he's on a different wavelength to what you consider is best for the DoH. Unfortunately, we have no idea where Dawson is located in the DoH building, so we cannot see what he's up to, which means we are limited as to what we can do," advised Paul.

"I can see what's preventing you from helping me. Leave the task of finding where he is hiding to me," suggested Sam.

They had finished their lunch and returned to Sam's office, they had about fifteen minutes before the chauffeur would arrive to take them back to the DoH building.

"Sam, we seem to be at a bit of an impasse. We are not entirely clear as to what you want from us and unclear as to what you are expecting us to get from Dawson. I think we need a clarification of what is going on," Caroline demanded, "either that or we are going to walk away from this."

"Does this apply to you as well, Paul?" Sam enquired.

"Why would it not, Sam?" Paul demanded, "Or perhaps you're trying to divide and conquer?"

"No, no, I'm not trying anything like that," Sam expressed in a subdued voice.

"If that is the case," Paul insisted, "then the time for subterfuge and games is over. Do you understand?" "Yes."

Suddenly the chauffeur came in and interrupted.

"Will it be alright if you pick up Paul and Caroline from the DoH building at nine o'clock in the morning? So we can continue this discussion," Sam asked the chauffeur. He nodded in agreement.

A little later, Paul and Caroline were sitting in their office.

"I wonder what is going on between Sam and Dawson." Paul asked Caroline rhetorically.

"I'm not sure I want to be involved with them anymore myself," Caroline acknowledged.

"Well, there's going to be a general election this coming Thursday. Consequently, I suggest that we listen to what is going to be said tomorrow, at Sir Gerard's office, but don't make any commitments until after the election, and we find out who the new Health Minister is going to be," suggested Paul. "Meanwhile, I think we'll go to your flat after we finish work this evening and examine those documents we have accumulated and see if we can establish anything that will give us some insight as to their relationship."

"That seems to be a good idea, Paul. I'm just concerned we may be getting involved in something we don't stand a chance of extraditing ourselves from, in a favourable light."

After spending approximately seven hours going through their collection of documents at Caroline's flat, they returned home to Paul's flat. The next morning, they were taken to Sir Gerard's flat by his chauffeur. At Sam's request, they settled themselves in the plush furniture of his flat.

"Help yourselves to champagne," Sam proffered, "we are just waiting for the arrival of Mr Dawson."

"Sam, where exactly does Mr Dawson work?"

"I don't know. All I do know, is that he is connected with personnel security in some way," recounted Sam.

The three of them sat in silence for about five minutes, until there was a knock on the door of Sam's flat. Mr Dawson came in response to Sam's summons to enter.

"Good morning, Keith, this is Paul Enfield and Caroline Aston; come and join us," Sam introduced them. "Paul and Caroline have been doing some research for me, and your name has come up, and they would like to know a bit more about you, if that is alright with you, Keith."

"Thank you, Sam. I have met Paul before, but I haven't met Caroline, although her reputation as a no-nonsense person has gone before her. What exactly do you both want to know?" Keith enquired.

"Firstly, we feel that it would help our research if we knew where you worked or were based," Paul explained, and also the relationship between you and Sir Gerard.

"Dealing with the first question first," asserted Mr Dawson. You will find that although I am seen in DoH buildings quite frequently, I'm actually based in Whitehall. As for the second part, I don't think it is any of your business.

"If that is also the view of Sir Gerard, then we shall be leaving this office at once. What is your view, Sir Gerard?" Paul enquired, in a voice that made the hair on the back of Sir Gerard's neck stand up.

Gerard stared at Paul.

"Sir Gerard, do you agree with Mr Dawson? A simple yes or no will do!" Paul exclaimed.

"No, I don't," responded Sir Gerard.

Chapter 25

Sir Gerard's flat fell deathly silent for several minutes after Sam's reply to Paul's question. The silence was eventually broken by Mr Dawson.

"Sir Gerard, in view of your answer to Paul's question, am I correct in assuming that you will no longer be supporting me in my drive to sell the National Health's vast amount of data to the Americans?"

"I'm afraid that I won't be supporting you, Keith, in your endeavour to make a vast amount of money for your political friends," Sir Gerard announced.

"In that case, I shall leave this office and go back to Whitehall and politely request you do not try to contact me," Mr Dawson declared, in a voice that indicated his declaration was final.

He walked over to the door and promptly left.

"Well," Sam said, "that's the end of that interesting escapade. I don't know what you two are going to do now, but if you need to gain access to the Whitehall computer system, I have a terminal you can use over in my office do you want to go over there now?"

"Good, but we need to go and create a plan of attack first now we know what we are fighting against, However, we shall be back to use your computer," Paul expounded.

"Please come and have lunch before you go," Sam entreated.

"Sam, I think that's the best idea you've had all morning," Caroline said patronisingly.

With that, the three of them got up and started to make their way over to the restaurant. Once they were seated and their meal had arrived, they looked inquiringly at Sam.

"The way you're looking at me, seems to indicate that you want me to open the conversation. Well, now that Mr Dawson has shown us his hand, we know where we are going, is that correct?" Sam said, opening the conversation.

"Let's consider the fact that there is going to be an election on Thursday," Paul acknowledged. "Which means there probably won't be a working health secretary until the following Monday, at the very earliest. Consequently, the general populace will not know what his thoughts concerning how the National Health is going to be run until sometime after that. Will Mr Dawson have access to the new health secretary before then? If so, we will need to do the same hence, would you have access to the health secretary?"

"Sam was Mr Dawson involved in any way with the AIDS fiasco?" interjected Caroline.

"Caroline, unfortunately, I don't know if he was involved in the AIDS cover-up. I hadn't thought that he might have been, but there is a possibility that he was, particularly if there was money to be made out of it. I will try and get a look at the financial records," Sam responded.

"Sam, please would you ask your chauffeur to come and pick us up in the morning, so that Caroline can have a rummage in the Whitehall computer?" Paul suggested.

"I can see no reason why the chauffeur can't," Sam replied.

They arrived back at the DoH entrance in Victoria Street.

"Caroline, I want to go and have a chat with Major Smithson about the security of that back door; do you want to come?" asked Paul.

"Of course I do."

By this time, they had arrived outside the security office. Paul knocked on the door, and they both entered.

"Please could we see Major Smithson," Paul asked the secretary. "I'll just phone and find out. Yes, he will see you now."

"Thank you."

With that, Paul knocked on the inner door, and both of them went in.

"And what can I do for the both of you?" inquired Major Smithson.

"It's nothing to worry about, just a question about security. We discovered a doorway the other day, when Caroline and I walked along Victoria Street and turned down the narrow road and found a door that had the signage 'DoH Maintenance' on it. We then tried to open it, expecting it to be locked. However, we were astounded when it did open onto a dimly lit corridor," described Paul. When we returned to our office, we looked on the map that is given to new starters and found where the back door was, which led out to the narrow road running down the side of this building.

Subsequently, we located the corridor leading to the outside door.

There were two doors leading to the corridor, one marked 'Workshop' and another marked 'Computer Room', which was also unlocked. Our question is, why is it so easy for someone to come in from the outside and gain access to one of our computers without any kind of security challenge? In fact, they could gain access to any part of this building.

"Can you show me this door?" asked Smithson, whose face had a look of disbelief.

"Yes, it will only take a few moments, come on," urged Paul.

They left the security office and walked along the main corridor until they came to a door marked 'Authorised personnel only'. Paul opened it.

"This is the corridor that leads to the outer door," explained Paul.

They continued along to the outer door, which Paul opened and led them outside into the narrow lane.

"I wouldn't have believed it if you hadn't shown me," Smithson gasped, with his mouth open. "I'm going back to my office to organise getting this door sealed."

"We'll come with you, just in case there is some problem about it having been authorised to be left open," Paul insisted.

When they arrived back in Smithson's office, Smithson's boss was contacted and enlightened about the serious lack of security. He then contacted the company that was responsible for the security of the building. Ten minutes later, the company phoned back and stated that they had received a letter dated five years ago stating that a particular door was to remain unlocked at all times. It was authorised by Mr

Dawson, who stated he was an executive of the DoH. Smithson's boss immediately contacted the security firm, who was informed that particular door must immediately be sealed permanently closed, indefinitely. If a request to revoke this situation is received, then a confirmation of said request must be approved from Mr Paul Enfield and Sir Gregory before being implemented.

We left Major Smithson to worry about the implementation of getting the door sealed and returned back to our office. As arranged, the next morning we arrived at Sir Gerard's office in Whitehall.

"Come in, you two, and make yourselves comfortable," Sam responded to their knock on the door.

"Good morning, Sam," greeted Paul and Caroline.

"I have assumed, as you'll be working, consequently coffee will be the drink of choice this morning."

"Yes, please, Sam, you've assumed correctly. By the way, do you have a printer in this office that is accessible from your Whitehall terminal?" Caroline asked.

"Yes, it's over there, on the small table next to the terminal," responded Sam.

"Good, I'll go and make a start," Caroline said, going over to the Whitehall terminal and switching it on. "Sam, do you want me to use your login, or make one up for myself?"

"Make one up for yourself, please," responded Sam, "then security won't come asking questions, and I can deny any knowledge of what is going on."

Silence descended over the office, apart from the clatter of Caroline working at the keyboard, which lasted for approximately ten minutes, until the printer sprang into life. Paul shot out of his chair and started examining the printer's output, which consisted of five letters, all addressed to Mr Dawson.

"This is interesting," Paul suddenly exclaimed, "this letter was sent by yourself, Sam. Do you want to comment about it before I read it in detail? It's dated about a week or so before the AIDS fiasco."

"If I remember correctly," Sam started to explain, his voice having a note of insecurity, "it was my thoughts about whether or not the isolation of AIDS victims on small islands was ethically right in this day and age. Unfortunately, at that point in time, Dawson was all for keeping them isolated. What his views are now, I have no idea."

"Well done, Sam; that is the basic thrust of your letter's content," Paul commended. "However, the contents of the other four letters are not in agreement with your views. In fact, a couple of them are suggesting a rather more violent end to AIDS victims than isolation."

"This next batch of documents is from a different directory with a higher level of security than those you have just read," announced Caroline.

The printer started spewing documents again this time there were twelve of them. Paul started to quickly scan them.

"These are a whole higher level of seriousness. In fact, I'm not going to let you read them, Sam, until I have finished analysing them."

"I have finished rummaging through the computer, for the time being anyway," Caroline suddenly divulged.

"Good," said Sam, "we can go to lunch."

"That's good; we've been waiting for you to make that suggestion," Paul and Caroline acquiesced.

Later, back in their office, Paul and Caroline started analysing what the documents from Whitehall implied for the future of the DoH.

Chapter 26

"We should know on Monday who is going to be the new Health Minister," Caroline pointed out. "And, it shouldn't be long after that when it's disclosed what he hopes to do with the National Health, regarding funding and the source of the money needed to realise his ambitions."

"I think the best thing we can do at the moment is to assume the worst, and devise a plan ready to implement if they decide to sell the National Health's personal data to the Americans. What do you think, Paul?"

"That is a good idea; we can start on it the morning, back in the office," Paul assented.

"Shall we do it like the AIDS disclosure?" Paul suggested.

"I'm not sure it will have the same impact, as nothing has actually been implemented; I think it would be passed off as an inconvenience and nothing will be achieved," Caroline challenged.

Suddenly, Paul's phone went off.

"Hello, Paul Enfield speaking…Mike, how nice to hear from you. Are you keeping well? What do you mean, what more chaos am I involved in? We would love to come and have a really good chinwag. Yes, there will be two of us.

Where are we to meet you? We know where that restaurant is. We will see you there Saturday, at six o'clock."

"Who was that?" demanded Caroline.

"Mike Elliot, we are going for a party at the restaurant in Victoria Station's concourse."

"Who is he?" asked Caroline.

"He was employed as the doctor when I was on that island in the Atlantic, and before you ask, he hasn't got AIDS," Paul clarified, "you meet him at Stansted Airport."

They continued to assemble which letters and documents would have the biggest and best impact on Sir Gerard. With the aim of getting rid of Mr Dawson and his backers, or at least neutralising them, regarding their attempts to influence the DoH's future.

Saturday afternoon dragged round until it was time for Paul and Caroline to leave for their much-anticipated party. They had decided to book a taxi for the journey to Victoria Station's concourse so as to arrive fresh and unsullied by the alternative walk.

The taxi dropped them off as close to the restaurant as possible, which left them about fifty metres to walk. When they arrived at the entrance, the doorman asked for their names.

"Paul Enfield and Caroline Aston," replied Paul.

"Your places are reserved on table five," the doorman responded.

"I expected a small group this sounds quite large," Paul asked in an inquiring voice.

"I have a list of twenty, sir."

"Thank you for letting us know."

"He's rather on the large side for a doorman, more of a bouncer, I would have thought," Paul whispered in Caroline's ear as they walked into the dining area.

"There's Mike waving at us," Paul announced, and the two of them walked over to the table where he was seated, which, by coincidence, was number five.

"Hello Mike, I think you have met Caroline."

"Yes, we meet at Stansted, which seems to have been a long time ago now," Mike observed.

"I don't know about you, Mike, but I was expecting a small intimate get together," Paul declared.

"So was I when Sir Gerard suggested it and asked me to contact you two," Mike explained.

"Is Sir Gerard here?" Asked Paul.

"Not as far as I know, I thought I was the first one to arrive," Mike confirmed.

"What do you think of him, Sir Gerard, I mean."

"Well, he helped me to get established in St Thomas's Hospital after I had finished organising the AIDS patients." Mike explained.

"Yes, we found him really helpful when we made public all those documents, which proved the government was behind the AIDS Island's fiasco," Paul explained.

"So, it was you, Paul, who got me a real hospital."

"With a little help, no, an exceedingly large amount of help from Caroline. Have you heard the name of our new department, 'The Unresolved Department'?"

"Through the Grapevine, I have heard what your department has achieved, but I didn't know it was your department."

Mike and Paul started to reminisce over their stay on the island in the Atlantic. Consequently, Caroline started to people watch the various members of the assembly as they gathered into the room.

Suddenly, she noticed someone surrounded by about six others.

"Paul, come down from putting the world to rights, and look at the table over in the far-left corner; do you recognise who it is at the centre?" Caroline insisted.

"Yes, it's Mr Dawson, what's he doing here?" Paul suddenly questioned.

As Paul rhetorically asked the question Sir Gerard suddenly sat in the chair next to him.

"Paul, that's the very question, I was going to ask," Sir Gerald said, with a tone of concern in his voice.

"Sam, I was expecting a more intimate gathering, than this, so what has happened?" inquired Paul. "The doorman looks more like a nightclub bouncer than a doorman, and most of the other attendees I do not recognise, apart from Mr Dawson, that is."

"Paul, it was originally intended to be a small gathering of about ten persons from your and the other AIDS Islands in the Atlantic. However, as the days, progressed, I was made aware that Mr Dawson was intent on inviting a group of his backers I suddenly realised that he was intending to generate a situation that would make it extremely difficult for me to remain employed by the DoH. Consequently, I had a secret meeting with the owners of this restaurant. Who suggested we let it run as if we hadn't realised what was liable to happen, and they would make appropriate adjustments to the personnel attendees, i.e., like the doorman."

"But Sam, from what you are saying, it seems that you are expecting this get together to end up in some kind of disruption."

"You are correct as usual," Sam continued, "out of the corner of my eye, I can see it's about to kick off—Mr Dawson is on the move."

"Quick, Caroline, take Sam and get a taxi to our flat; don't look at Dawson, and make sure a neighbour sees you go into the flat. Go on, do it now!"

Caroline and Sir Gerard got out of their seats and rushed out of the main door.

A few seconds later, Mr Dawson arrived at table five.

"Where have those two gone?" Dawson demanded.

"Mind your own business," Paul snapped back.

By now, the six men who had been sitting with Dawson had also arrived at table five.

"One of you men, go and find out where Gerard and that woman have gone, and bring them back here," Dawson commanded. The man rushed towards the main door, but the doorman had got there before him and locked it. The man rushed up and took a swipe at the doorman. However, the doorman, who was obviously expecting some kind of aggression, landed the first punch, and the man collapsed onto the floor.

By now, a group of the other guests had encircled Dawson and the other five men, informing them they were policeman, and promptly arrested them.

"Enfield, I'll make you pay for this!" Dawson suddenly bellowed.

"What, like you made all those AIDS patients, you marooned on those islands in the Atlantic Ocean, until they died," retorted Paul.

"You can't prove any of that nonsense," Dawson shouted, but his voice had a note of fear in it.

"I have enough hard evidence to put you and your money grabbing cronies away for a long time," Paul responded with a quiet voice and a smile on his face.

Dawson and his five remaining cronies were led out to a waiting police van. The one who had been floored by the doorman, next to the main door, had now recovered and was collected by the police on the way through. When the doorman was asked why he hit him, he said it was self-defence, and all the witnesses who had seen the event agreed.

"It turned out that some of the other guests were from the press, and from the accounts in the morning editions of their papers, they had had a field day."

Three days later, Caroline and Paul were sitting in Sir Gerard's office, drinking Sam's champagne.

"Sam, how did you find out that Dawson was going to discredit you?" asked Paul.

"The owner of the restaurant told me that Dawson was inquiring what dates I would next be in the restaurant. Dawson then insisted that the owner booked a table for him and six others. The owner didn't think there would be a problem, as their table was in a corner, out the way. A day or two later, I received information that Dawson was going to create a situation that would mean I would be removed for the DoH's employment. Consequently, I went and had a private chat with the owner, and we came up with the plan, in which you played a significant part, even though you didn't know anything about it," Sam recounted. "I see," Paul replied.

"But why did you suddenly dispatch me and Caroline to your flat?" Sam queried.

"Well, Sam, remember that Caroline and I had acquired a bundle of letters and documents, which unequivocally proved that Dawson was one of the main persons involved in the drive to get AIDS patients isolated on the islands. And also, why he wanted NHS patient data shipped to the USA."

"Hence, when Dawson started to move, I guessed it would involve you, which meant I had to get you out of the way and be able to prove you were somewhere else," Paul explained. "Now I have a question for you. What is going to happen to Dawson and his cronies?"

"The six businessmen who were representing the companies involved in making a considerable amount of money from the AIDS debacle and were anticipating doing the same if the American data transfer went ahead. Have had all their governmental contracts cancelled, with immediate effect."

"As for Mr Dawson, all his access to Whitehall and DoH buildings have been revoked he is also being investigated to establish what illegal activities he has been involved in."

"That seems reasonably comprehensive," Paul concurred.

"The champagne has all gone, so can we go to lunch now, please, Sam?" Caroline requested.

"Only if you promise not to suddenly drag me across London," Sam answered, with a huge smile on his face.

Their main course had just arrived when Paul suddenly asked Sam.

"Sam, as we have just solved yet another of your hidden agendas, what are you scheduling for us next?"

"Paul, I would suggest you and Caroline take a fortnight's holiday, or even longer if you wish, to enable the disruption you two have been instrumental in creating, has calmed down, and I can then establish the next potential problem for you to resolve." Sam suggested.

They had finished their meal and returned to Sam's office to await the chauffeur's return.

"O' by the way, Paul," Sam suddenly interjected, "an office in this block, which is only slightly smaller than mine, will become available shortly. Would you like me to put your name on it?"

"Yes, please. I assume that it will be as easy to excess from the great outdoors as yours is. Also with the proviso, that we can keep our old office in the archive department as well." responded Paul.

"That's fine, but why would you want two offices?" Queried Sam.

"So that you will never know where Caroline and I are at any given time. Also being involved on the shop floor will make gathering a different sort of information much easier."

"I have just had a thought," Paul suddenly announced, "that having an appealing regency decorated office of exquisite dimensions with a Whitehall address would enable 'The Unresolved Department' to widen its scope of operation to areas outside the 'DoH'. Perhaps we may even change its title to 'The Mayhem Department'."

"I see, I'm going to have to try and keep an eye on you two when you come back from holiday," Sam responded, with a big grin on his face.

"Another thought," Caroline added, "is when we move into our Whitehall office. Whose side will we belong to?"

"That may depend on who we are working for," Paul elucidated.

Chapter 27

When we returned from our holidays, several things had changed; the most significant one, for us anyway, was that we had married. However, in keeping with her temperate, Caroline refused to change her name from Ashton. Consequently, her name hasn't changed to Caroline Enfield but is still Caroline Ashton. At least, the signage on the office doors will not need changing.

Another change is that we potentially have two offices. Although we still have to see our posh second office.

We decided our first visit would be back at our original office in the general archiving area on the first floor.

"Good morning, Sue's Dragon," they announced as they arrived at her desk.

"This is a nice surprise, you are coming back; I mean, I didn't expect you to lower yourself by coming back up here," responded Sue's Dragon with a huge smile.

"How could we abandon some of our closest acquaintances?" Caroline responded, "Come round to our office in about half an hour, and bring Pratt as well if you want to."

With that, Paul and Caroline went into their office. There were a few letters to be dealt with, which Paul did whilst

Caroline booted her computer up and checked for messages. Neither of them found anything requiring their immediate response.

A few moments later, Sue's Dragon and David Pratt knocked on the door and entered.

"Come in you two and sit down," requested Paul. "I'm expecting you would like to let us know what has happened whilst we have been away."

"Well, it's been very calm and peaceful here, since you have not been around," mooted David Pratt, smiling at the pair of them.

"Yes, it's been very quiet and settled," agreed Sue's Dragon.

"All very droll, I'm sure. Anyway, the main change for us is that we have got married. However, in line with Caroline's stubbornness, she has refused to change her name to Enfield, which means, in a funny sort of way, nothing's changed."

"Congratulations on your matrimony; we both hope you will be very happy," Sue's Dragon answered.

"And we know now who the boss is in your family," added David.

"Thank you for your kind wishes. However, having worked with Paul, I think he is who will be the one in charge," explained Caroline.

"I think I'll give it a few months before I agree with that," Sue's Dragon acquiesced.

"The other thing that has changed is that we will have another office over in Whitehall, although we haven't seen it yet," Paul announced, "we agreed to take the Whitehall office on the agreement that we could also keep this office," Paul clarified, "Why do you want two offices?" David inquired.

"Because, as I told the inquisitor who gave us the option of the second office, nobody will really know, which office we are working in at any given time," Paul explained, grinning.

"So you will still be causing mayhem as you have done before, but we won't know when it's going to happen," observed Sue's Dragon.

"Just keeping you on your toes, but we will still be coming around to see you," Caroline expounded, "just to keep you wondering."

The room filled with laughter. Suddenly, amid all the humour, Paul's phone started ringing.

"Paul Enfield Speaking," Paul answered the phone, "yes, we'll be down directly, thank you."

Turning to the others in the room, Paul announced, "Caroline and myself have been summoned to go to Sir Gerard's, hopefully to see our second office. Please excuse us, and thank you for our wonderful welcome back from holiday."

Sir Gerard's chauffeur was waiting in the foyer as normal. It wasn't long before we were sitting in Sir Gerard's office.

"Did you have a nice holiday?" Sam asked.

"I was wonderful, and there is one thing we need to tell you, and that is that we are now married."

"How did that happen?" Sam queried.

"We stopped a Gretna Green on our way through Scotland."

"As simple as that?"

"Well, no, we had to do some preparation work first," Caroline confessed.

"So, you have changed your name, Caroline?"

"No, she hasn't; she refused," declared Paul. "so nothing has changed regarding names, except she is now a Mrs."

"I'll agree with you two that nothing's changed you always managed to do the totally unexpected," Sam illuminated. "Right, having sorted that out, would you like to come and see your new Whitehall home." "Yes please!" Paul and Caroline responded in unison.

They left Sam's office and crossed to the other side of the main staircase, and there were a pair of double doors. Sam took a bunch of keys out of his pocket and handed them to Paul.

"There you are now open your new office."

Paul inserted the key and turned it, then pushed the doors open.

"Wow!" exclaimed Caroline. "It's beautiful."

"You have got two desks with swivel chairs, a sofa, and two armchairs, plus half a dozen hardback chairs, as well as assorted computer terminals." Sam catalogued for them.

"Have we got a phone each?" Caroline asked.

"Yes, but only one number."

"What is the postal address to get here?" Paul inquired.

"Here's a box of business cards with the name of your department, with its address and phone number."

"I see this office is called the Blue Office," Caroline noticed. "Is that because of the blue regency decoration?"

"Basically yes, in addition, this card has got George my chauffeur's phone number on it, who you can use to get between here and the DoH building and visa-versa. I think that is everything. Is it to your satisfaction?" Sam summarised.

"Yes, thank you. If it's not, we know where you live. Now, Sam, please come over to my desk and show me which button to press to get a bottle of champagne and how to book a table in the restaurant."

"I wondered how long it would be before we got round to the booze," remarked Sam, walking over to one of the desks. "You see this box here with three push buttons, the middle one connects you with the person who provides the drinks, etc., and the first one connects you to your private secretary (who is also mine). Go on then, Paul, order your champagne, and don't forget the glasses," Sam instructed.

Eventually, the champagne arrived with its three attendant glasses.

"So you are Paul Enfield and Caroline Aston, the new custodians of the Blue Office," the young lady bringing the drink in observed.

"And your name is?" Caroline queried.

"I'm called Rosaline, amongst other things," she smiled back, and then left the office.

Sam opened the bottle of champagne and filled the three glasses.

"Please help yourselves."

They started drinking.

"Here's to your happy occupation of this office," proposed Sam.

"Thank you, Sam, for organising our occupation of this office," announced Paul.

"It may be a few weeks before another job raises its ugly head for you both to get your teeth into," Sam explained. "So I shall now leave you to enjoy your new office."

"O' just before you go, Sam, this is my personal number," Paul handed Sam a piece of paper with a phone number on it.

"Thank you, Paul."